MURDER IN THE POE ROOM

MURDER IN THE POE ROOM

Mary Alice Gunter

Library of Congress Number: 2002096651
ISBN : Softcover 1-4010-8884-8

This is a work of fiction. Names, characters, places and incidents either are the product of the author's imagination or are used fictitiously, and any resemblance to any actual persons, living or dead, events, or locales is entirely coincidental.

This book was printed in the United States of America.

To order additional copies of this book, contact:
Xlibris Corporation
1-888-795-4274
www.Xlibris.com
Orders@Xlibris.com
17498

DISCLAIMER

All the characters in this novel are fictitious, and any resemblance to a person living or dead is purely coincidental. The University of Virginia is the setting for this story because the Poe Room is located here, and the traditions of the University, such as the Honor Code, are factual. However, most of the administrative positions referred to do not exist. There is no chancellor or director of historical preservation. There has never been a murder in the Poe Room or in the tunnels. The writer intends no disrespect for the history or traditions of the University..

MAIN CHARACTERS IN ORDER OF APPEARANCE

Ellen Randolph: Historical Director of the University
Robert Randolph: Ellen's husband, deceased, who was Chairman of the English Department.
Mark Pace: Chief of the University Police
Jake Shifflett: Chief of the County Police
Charlie Allan: Student found murdered in the Poe Room
Henry Dodson: Member of the secret society who mysteriously disappeared after being accused of blackmail
Frank Gruver: Member of the secret society; real estate developer; husband of Anne
John Grieco: Member of the secret society; a lawyer running for state senator
Anthony Antonetti: Member of the secret society; deceased
George Blake: Member of the secret society; a judge
Ted Mitchell: Member of the secret society; dean of the college
Bowman Ward: Vice Chancellor of the University
Fannie Groomes: Ellen's friend; a domestic
Reverend George Evans: Episcopal priest; father of Anne and grandfather of Sarah
Lydia Evans: Wife of Reverend Evans and mother of Anne
Etta Mae Toliver: Fannie's sister; a domestic
Anne Gruver: Wife of Frank Gruver and daughter of Reverend Evans and Lydia Evans
Dexter Paine: Chief of the City Police
Susan Ames: Reference librarian
Hiram Perkins: Reference librarian
Alice Fenton: Student

Rebecca Mitchell: Wife of the dean of the college, Ted Mitchell
Tom Peters: Cousin to Fannie; retired from the staff of the country club
Martin Harrison: Retired professor of English
Arnold Harrison: Nephew of Martin
Sarah Collins: Daughter of Anne Gruver
Bennett Collins: Sara's husband

CHAPTER ONE

... They have nearly finished the Rotunda—The pillars of the Portico are completed and it greatly improves the appearance of the whole—The books are removed into the library—and we have a very fine collection ...

Letter of Edgar Allan Poe, September 1826

It was early morning in Virginia on a spring day that promised to feel more like August by the afternoon. The scent of wisteria was heavy in the warm air, and the children's sneakers were soaked from the damp grass. The boy and girl ran through the arcades of Mr. Jefferson's original academic village at the University of Virginia shrieking with pleasure, dodging in and out of the early 19th-century pillars.

The children lived in one of the faculty pavilions on the Lawn—that part of the central Grounds of the University designed and built under the personal direction of Thomas Jefferson, or *Mister* Jefferson as he is affectionately and continuously referred to at the University. It was as though he still lived on Monticello Mountain, overlooking the town, ready to gallop down on a moment's notice if he saw something that displeased him.

The boy ran ahead of his sister and then waited for her in ambush behind the columns and shrubbery. The little girl, in wild pursuit, rounded the gravel drive leading to the West Range and halted suddenly before the Edgar Allen Poe room. She pressed her nose against the plexiglass that allowed visitors to see into the historically popular site. The boy appeared from his hiding place, some distance ahead, and called to her, but she did not move from the spot.

"What's the matter with you? Come on," the boy called. But still she did not move.

"There's somebody sleeping in Mr. Poe's bed," she said.

"Sure there is," he jeered, "and his horse is tied over there at the library." "Hey, come on! We're going to be late for school."

"But there really is," she pleaded. "He's all scrunched up with the blanket over him."

"You know what mom said would happen if we're late again."

Reluctantly, the little girl turned and slowly followed her brother.

* * *

It was several hours later before Herman and Ida Holcomb from South Bend, Indiana, made the same discovery. Since exams were over and many students had left the Grounds, most of the rooms were empty, so there was little foot traffic in the colonnade in front of the Poe room.

"Herman, there's something funny looking about that bed. I believe there is someone asleep in there." Ida strained her eyes to see through the plexiglass door, on which the light was casting a glare.

Herman, who was punching the button that was supposed to deliver a message about Edgar Allan Poe, but as usual, was out of order, peered into the room. "I think it must be a pile of covers. Maybe someone forgot to make the bed."

"No, I 'm certain there is someone in that bed. I think I can see his hair, which seems to be red, and a hand outside the covers. And there on the floor—that looks like a wine bottle and a glass turned over. Do you think he could be drunk?"

"Well, it wouldn't surprise me any, considering how they party here. Hey, maybe we have the wrong place and we are staring into some student's bedroom."

"Oh, for heaven's sake, Herman, they don't put plexiglass doors on student rooms so that tourists can look in. And see that big raven over there sitting in the window? Of course this is the Poe room. Here, I'll just knock on the panel and see if I can wake him up."

"I think we should go on and mind our own business." Herman began to move away, pulling on his wife's arm.

"No, Herman, he isn't moving. This just doesn't look right to me. There is something wrong with that boy."

The campus police, parked in front of the library across the road from the Poe Room, were reluctant at first to attend to Ida's concern.

"Well, ma'am, it's probably just a shadow or something that you are seeing."

"Yeah, that's what I told her, officer." Herman was trying to maneuver his wife toward their car, which he had illegally parked down the block.

But Ida was adamant and, finally, it was a most bewildered traffic patrol officer who called headquarters to announce that someone was sleeping in Mr. Poe's bed—and sleeping very soundly indeed!

CHAPTER TWO

All that we see or seem
Is but a dream within a dream . . .
—Poe's "A Dream Within A Dream"

On nice days Ellen Randolph ate her lunch sitting on a bench in the garden of the Colonnade Club, a pavilion on the Lawn reserved for the use of the faculty. The peonies and roses were a blaze of color against the soft greenery. As usual, she ate alone, taking only a short time away from her duties as the historical director of the University. Her department was located on the lower floor of the historic Rotunda, and this time of the year, after classes were over, visitors came there frequently for tours and information. It had been a busy morning, with tourists and prospective students arriving in a steady flow.

A squirrel edged his way closer to her foot in hopes of a crust and was rewarded with a generous portion. Ellen laughed at his antics, as he scampered away from his chattering relatives to gobble his prize. Once she had found squirrels to be a common nuisance, but now she found them entertaining and good company. She sympathized with those who put out elaborate bird feeders, only to see the squirrels devour both the seeds and the feeders, but she admired the cleverness and determination of these agile creatures. She loved to watch as they sailed through the tree tops and tightrope-walked their way across telephone lines.

Today, with the gardens full of flowers, she thought of the time when she and other faculty wives had acted as volunteer guides, leading visitors through the Grounds in hushed and reverential tones. They would describe the architecture of the University of Virginia and share discreet tidbits of genteel gossip about the history of some of the early residents of the hallowed Grounds. They particularly enjoyed telling the story of the duels fought by students in the early years, or the fact that cows often poked their heads through the open windows of the classrooms, to the dismay of the bewigged professors.

She had memorized the words to the talk she gave and could hear her own voice speaking in those soft, genteel southern tones she seemed to have lost over the years. Truth to say, part of the accent had been "put on" for the benefit of the visitors, to satisfy their image of the typical "Virginia Lady." Some of the guides even added downcast eyes, fluttery hand movements, and liberal dabbings with a lace handkerchief to their performance.

"You are standing on the Lawn, which is the tree-lined central quadrangle of the old Grounds of the University of Virginia designed by our own Mr. Jeffahson," she would begin. "The magnificent Rotunda stands at one end of the Lawn with buildings gracefully attached on both sides, arches and colonnades facing each other in puhfect symmetry. Certain privileged faculty members, deans, depahtment chairs or chaired professors of note, are invited to live in the faculty residences, called pavilions, which are part of this group of buildings, with each pavilion representing a different version of a classical style of architecture."

At this point, she would always lower her head modestly and inform the admiring assemblage that she was privileged to live in "that lovely pavilion just ovah theah, since my husband is the chairman of the English depahtment." (She loved the little oohs and ahs that accompanied that announcement.) After a genteel pause and clearing of the throat, she would continue.

"The low, single rooms linking the pavilions on each side of the Lawn are individual rooms, highly sought after by student leaders in the fourth-year class willing to put up with the inconvenience of the—ah—facilities located beneath the buildings and accessible only by goin' outside and around the back. On cold winter mornings, students can be seen scurryin' through the snow in their bathrobes." At this point, she would cough modestly and hurriedly move on, intimating that some half-clad student might suddenly appear.

"The two rows of student housing running parallel to the Lawn, and identical to the Lawn rooms, are called the East and West Ranges. In the 19th century, as the University grew, the ranges were constructed to house the overflow of students from the Lawn. Now, these rooms are resuhved for graduate students willing to put up with the inconveniences of the old buildings for the onnah of their historical ambience."

She would lead the group down the graveled path between the serpentine walls, pointing out the uniqueness of their design, until they came to the West Range. "One of the rooms on the West Range not open for graduate student residence is the Poe room—the room that housed Edgar Allen Poe in 1826, when he was a student at the University. He originally lived on the Lawn, but after a dispute with his roommate, he moved to the West Range, which was then known as Rowdy Row. His room, number 13, has been turned into a mini-museum." At this point, she would give each of the visitors an opportunity to peer through the plexiglass door and listen to the recording about the young Edgar Allen Poe that came from a speaker above the door. Then she would lead them into the gardens.

"Behind each of the pavilions on the Lawn is a gahden tended by the groundskeepers of the University. In Jeffersonian times, the gahdens on the East range were primarily for fruit trees and the gahdens on the West were for vegetables, thus serving the utilitarian purposes of providing food for the students. Now, all of the gahdens, full of flowers and flowering shrubs and trees, are used for receptions and parties or for strollin' about or just sitting on the bench."

Just sitting on the bench, as I am doing now, she thought. The time when that southern lady walked through the "gahdens" leading those tours was long ago, and the woman who sat folding her lunch bag and shaking out a few last crumbs for the sparrows before returning to work was a very different person.

In that once orderly and serene universe, she could still see herself moving as in a warm transparent aura full of sunlight and roses. After the tour, there would have been lunch with some of the other wives, at the local country club or in one of the gardens, and then a quiet afternoon nap or a stroll with her daughter. She could imagine the little girl's blond curls bouncing above the flowers as she scurried along the path playing hide and seek, or when she was older, sitting on the bench and telling of the day's adventures in school. Often, Robert would join them, sitting in the afternoon sun, recounting the day's events and making her laugh at his gentle mockery of some of his arrogant colleagues.

She had loved Robert from the first time they met at a reception on the Lawn. He was an assistant professor in the English department at the University and she was a junior at Mary Baldwin College for Women in Staunton, Virginia. One of her professors had invited a few students to accompany him to the University to hear a lecture by William Faulkner and there had been a reception following in the faculty club.

Ellen had been standing alone, feeling awed by the presence of the great writer and insignificant in the company of University of Virginia faculty, all of whom seemed so confident and learned, waving their wine glasses and cigarettes like scepters. Robert had appeared at her side with a glass of punch and said, "You look like you could use this. The atmosphere can get a little heavy when the faculty members are all trying to impress someone famous."

Ellen had smiled gratefully and looked into the greenest eyes she had ever seen. They seemed to be lit from some source within and then shaded by long, dark lashes. For a moment she was mesmerized. Then, she found her voice and replied, "Thank you. I do feel a little out of place."

At twenty, Ellen was taller than most of her friends and she had strong arms and shoulders from playing tennis. Most of her dainty friends urged her to dress to look more "feminine" and put a "nice perm" in her hair, but she found that she was only comfortable in plain, simple clothing, with her long auburn hair brushed back and held in place with a velvet ribbon.

"Are you a student?" she had asked him. And he had explained that he was a new faculty member, having just finished his Ph.D. at Harvard.

"I haven't been here long enough to be part of the group, and everyone still treats me like a student since I did my undergraduate work here. Sometimes I feel like eighteen, instead of twenty-eight."

At that moment, William Faulkner had walked across the room and placed his hand on Robert's shoulder. In a voice loud enough to be heard by the entire assemblage he had said, "Young man, I read your article in the journal. I don't like most things that are written about my work. In fact, I don't read most things written about me, but a friend told me I should read this article. It was excellent! You are a very perceptive scholar—and those two words don't usually go together, in my opinion."

Then, without another word, the great man had turned on his heels and left the room. From that moment on, Robert was neither taken for granted nor treated like a student by his colleagues again.

They had married three months after her graduation. She was twenty-two and he was thirty—a rising star in the department. Two years later, he was made department chairman, and soon after the birth of their daughter, they had gone to live in the pavilion on the Lawn. She had taught him to play tennis, to enjoy mysteries, hot curry, and Vivaldi. He had taught her to love long walks in the mountains, fine wine and William Blake, bird dogs and Brahms. He taught her many things, except how to find joy without him.

CHAPTER THREE

. . . You have no doubt heard of the disturbances in College—Soon after you left here the Grand Jury met and put the students in a terrible fright—so much so that the lectures were unattended—and those whose names were upon the Sheriff's list—traveled off into the woods & mountains—taking their beds and provisions along with them . . .

Letter of Edgar Allan Poe, May 1826

For a few moments, as she walked back to her office in the Rotunda, she felt herself to be in that once magic space, the smell of lilac blooms in the air, the gentle hum of the bees, and the sound of a mockingbird high in the oak tree. Abruptly, the mood was broken by a student calling to her from one of the rooms. "Hi, Mrs. Randolph, how goes it?"

"Very well, Carl, thank you." She waved at the young man, tanning himself in a chair in the doorway of his room on the Lawn. Her voice was crisp and direct, with only a faint trace of a Southern drawl. "Be careful of the sun, or you'll look like a lobster for your graduation." Ellen enjoyed the students. Most of them were bright and worked hard. For those students who had too much money and too little discipline, she felt pity. They were throwbacks to the time when the University was primarily for rich and privileged white males. Ellen often wondered what Mr. Jefferson, with his enlightened views on the perfectability of human nature, had thought about the "gentlemen" at his new university spending so much of their time in drunken and disorderly behavior.

The admission of African-American students and then women to the College of Arts and Sciences in the late 60's and early 70's had greatly improved the academic environment. Ellen remembered the bitter accusations and predictions regarding the downfall of the University as a result of the arrival of these "unwanted interlopers," as some had referred to them.

Ellen often remembered with shame her own jealousy when Robert had spoken publicly in favor of women being admitted to the college. She had been embarrassed when some of the other faculty wives had made sly comments and veiled allusions to his interest in having those disgraceful "young females" in class. She could not believe that she could have been so provincial and so blind as to fail to understand his courage in standing up for the rights of these young people. Fortunately, she had kept her thoughts to herself; and Robert seemed unaware of her reactions.

Many times over the years when she had faced condescension and discrimination as a woman working in a man's world, she had touched her locket and thought of Robert's words as he spoke out about the rights of women. He had predicted that the admission of African-American students and women to all parts of the University on an equal status would propel the school into the ranks of major universities, and he had been so right. He had predicted that someday these individuals would take their places as leaders in the institution, and he had been right about that, also. It did not occur to her that if Robert had lived, she might never have become one of those leaders.

Before going into her office, which was just off of the display area in one of the ground floor rooms of the Rotunda, she checked the afternoon assignments for the student volunteers who had replaced faculty wives as guides and then wiped the glass cases where historical papers and artifacts were kept, should there be any fingerprints from the morning's group of visitors. The magnolia leaves in the Chinese vase in the window were still beautiful, with their waxy luster, and the 18-century furniture in this room glowed in the early afternoon light.

After twenty-seven years, she had become almost as much a part of the University as the Grecian columns and the statue of Mr. Jefferson on the main floor of the Rotunda. She had taken a position as assistant to the historical director in 1973. Although she knew little then about historical preservation, the offer had come from the kindheartedness of the chancellor of the University during a series of disasters in her life, the memories of which could still make time unravel around the edges.

She had found, to her own surprise and to the surprise of many who knew her, that she had a talent for the careful organization and attention to detail required by the job. Her connections with the first families of Virginia had proved to be a great boost to the fund-raising, an essential part of preservation.

Ellen checked her reflection in the glass of the grandfather clock, to make sure her hair was in place and that there were no wrinkles in the white blouse and dark pleated skirt. A large gold locket was her only jewelry. She touched the locket and felt the sense of loss and sorrow of memories that never completely went away, but also the happiness and love that were a part of those memories. She often got through difficult times by touching the locket and becoming for a moment a part of another time and place. However, the magic memories from the garden had to give way for the practical world of a woman who worked hard for a living and who had not had a nap after lunch on a workday for almost thirty years.

There were days like today, when Ellen was very aware of the time gone by and wondered what she would do about retirement, amazed that she had survived to be a part of the new millennium. Actually, sixty-three was not so old in a university where some tenured professors stayed on until they could barely creep across the Lawn, but she did not intend to remain too long. The demands of the job were beginning to wear on her, and with another capital campaign scheduled to begin in two years, she had no desire to travel and organize fund-raisers.

A visitor waiting in line for the tour of the Rotunda stared openly at the tall, handsome woman who moved with such authority through the crowd, stopping to speak to one of the student guides.

"Good afternoon, Pat. Are you ready for your first tour?" She smiled at the young woman waiting nervously for the clock to strike the hour.

"I think so, Mrs. Randolph. I have a few notes up my sleeve, just in case."

Like all of the student volunteers who led tours of the Rotunda, Pat was in awe of Ellen Randolph. It was not just the way Mrs. Randolph moved and spoke and her striking appearance, with that wonderful silver hair and dark blue eyes, but that she knew everybody and everybody knew and respected her. Deans spoke respectfully to Mrs. Randolph and professors went out of their way to win her approval. She had earned this respect as the University's historical director, a position to which she had been appointed when her predecessor retired. She had helped to turn the Grounds of the University into one of the most famous historical sites in America—and one of the most efficiently managed.

"Oh, Mrs. Randolph," Pat said, lowering her voice so that she would not be overheard in the crowded room. "Did you hear about the body they found in the Poe room this morning? It was that young man with the red hair who has been in here several times. They say he committed suicide in some really bizarre way. I'll have to skip that part of the tour because the road is closed and they are . . . ." Pat halted abruptly, since Mrs. Randolph was already moving rapidly towards her office, her heels clicking on the wooden floor.

Ellen Randolph picked up the phone on her desk and called the University police department. About one thing she was absolutely certain—this particular young man had not committed suicide.

CHAPTER FOUR

I saw fall within the goblet as if from some invisible spring in the atmosphere of the room three or four large drops of a brilliant ruby colored fluid.

—Poe's "Ligeia"

Mark Pace had been chief of the University police force only for a few months, and he found it took some getting used to. He had a way of getting through to people and winning their trust. However, at times, he still felt self-conscious and ill at ease with the wealthy, educated, and sophisticated people in this university community. He had grown up in Belmont, a part of the city that used to be on the wrong side of the tracks, before it became gentrified in the '80's by young professionals restoring the quaint Victorian homes. He had finished his classes in the community college by studying at night after working as a deputy in the university police department during the day. His mother had been a cook in food services at the University and his father a trainer at a local horse farm.

There was some grumbling by other candidates for the chief's position regarding Mark's appointment. Some insinuated that Mark had been favored by the vice chancellor of the University, Bowman Ward, because Mark was an excellent rider and his father trained the vice chancellor's horses. Mark believed he had earned the position by being careful and thorough in his work. The vice chancellor might admire his riding ability, but that didn't help solve cases or manage the department.

At thirty-eight, Mark was one of the youngest police chiefs in the area. Quiet and soft-spoken, he nevertheless commanded respect and authority. An extremely hard worker, who expected the same from those in his force, he was also known for his compassion and kindness. A number of young women would welcome some interest from the handsome chief, but he seemed oblivious to any such possibility. When suggestions to join a party or double date were made, he usually laughed and replied that he was too busy keeping the peace to join their escapades. In fact, he was still bruised after the failure of his marriage, and he spent most evenings alone in his small apartment or working in his office.

Mark stooped to enter the doorway of the small nineteenth-century room. The corpse was lying on the narrow bed, covered by an embroidered wool spread that was part of the permanent display. The red hair was bright against the striped ticking of the mattress and freckles stood out against the pallor of his skin. The man looked very young and vulnerable, with his face and body contorted from pain. One arm hung down over the edge of the bed, with fingers pointing towards an open bottle of wine on the floor beside the bed, together with an overturned glass. A dark stain of spilled wine was on the floor next to the glass. Mark had an uneasy feeling that the dead man was trying to indicate the source of his suffering. From the blue tinge of the fingernails, Mark assumed that the bottle of wine contained strychnine, but he would have to wait for the coroner's report to be sure.

Except for the presence of the corpse, the room appeared to be undisturbed. There was a small writing desk on which were stacked several old books, one of which was a copy of Poe's poems which was open to the "Raven." The line "Quoth the Raven Nevermore" had been underlined with a quill pen that was also a part of the regular display. Mark knew that ink was kept in the inkwell on the desk for meetings of the Raven Society, an honorary society whose members were formally inducted twice each year, when their names were signed into the membership book with the quill pen. The underlined words from the poem appeared to be a suicide message from the deceased. Mark looked at the dead man's hand and noted that there were ink stains on the fingers.

In addition to the bed and the table, there was also an antique hat box on the floor next to the chest, a fireplace, a chair, and a table used as a wash stand, on which there was a bowl and pitcher, and, perched on the window ledge, a life-size cast-iron statue of a raven, giving the eerie impression of staring with one cocked eye at the victim. A flashlight that apparently belonged to the deceased had rolled under the bed.

Mark's inspection was interrupted by the arrival of Jake Shifflett, the chief of police for Albemarle County. At six-foot-three, Jake had to stoop to get through the low door, and his burly presence seemed to fill the small room. Jake and Mark worked well together, sharing their limited resources and staff whenever it was necessary. Jake had six rambunctious children, and he and his round little wife, Molly, were always trying to fix Mark up with "a nice girl."

"How in the world do those tall basketball players ever fit into one of these spaces? They must have to fold themselves in half." Jake looked around the room curiously. "I can't figure out how the deceased got in here. The room was locked from the outside when we got here. I had to send someone to get the key from the administration building so we could get in. The window was locked from the inside and there didn't seem to be any sign of forced entry."

"Was there a key on the body?" Mark asked.

"No, and there isn't one in the room anywhere. He had to have found some way to get in, though, unless he slipped himself under the door."

"Let's have the men move everything in the room and see what the floor and walls look like," Mark said.

Jake called in two of the officers and they moved all of the furniture to the center of the room. Under a steamer trunk that stood beneath the window, they noticed that the flooring had been cut to make what appeared to be a crude trap door.

"Get something we can pry this up with," Mark ordered, and in a moment an officer returned with a thin file that slipped inside the crack and allowed the section of flooring to be lifted. The opening had evidently been cut to allow access from above to some of the plumbing and wiring under the room. There was a crude notched finger hold in the underside that someone had carved into the wood to allow the section to be pulled back into place from below.

"Why would anyone want to close the door from underneath this room?" Jake asked, scratching the permanent grey stubble on his chin. "If you used this trap door to get under the floor to check the plumbing and wiring, you should come back up the way you went down."

"There must be some place to go under here," Mark said, getting on his knees and peering into the opening with the flashlight. The trap door led into a crawl space, into which he gingerly lowered himself.

"Good thing you're nice and thin. They'd have to haul me out of there with a hoist." Jake leaned over and called anxiously into the opening, "What d'you see down there?" Mark's light had momentarily disappeared.

In a few moments, Mark called back to say that the crawl space opened into the service tunnel behind the Range. The service tunnels carried steam pipes throughout the campus in an interconnecting web and were large enough for a person to stand upright in most places. The tunnels could be accessed by way of ladders located inside manholes at various points around the Grounds.

Mark pulled himself back up into the room, dusting the dust from his trousers. "It would take very little effort to enter the tunnel through one of the manholes, climb down the ladder, proceed through the crawl space to the trap door, push it open from below and then climb into the room," he told Jake. "The students are always getting into those tunnels. We even found a homeless person living in one last year."

Mark examined the body again and pointed out the dirt on the knees of the trousers and under the nails. "I think that dirt indicates pretty clearly that he got into the room through the crawl space. It would appear that this was a case of suicide by poison, since he apparently was in this room alone." Shaking his head, he said, "Something about this scene just doesn't make any sense. Why would he come here?" Mark sat on the edge of the chair and looked around as though he could find some clue in the tiny room to the actions of the pale young man on the cot.

"Well, these poor kids can come up with some strange things. This time of the year we usually have one or two suicides of young folks, either here on the Grounds or in the community. A lot of times it's over something that would likely seem pretty trivial to them in a few years. I guess they just can't seem to see to the end of their misery." Jake was a kind man and the suffering he encountered often touched him deeply.

"I guess we better have the boys come in and take him away now, if that's all right with you, Mark. I'll let you know what the coroner says about the poison." Jake reached down and picked up the bottle of wine, carefully examining the label. "Hey, Mark, this is Amontillado wine. Isn't that the name of some Poe story? I remember reading it in high school."

Mark looked at the label again, carefully. "You're right, Jake. I think it was 'The Cask of the Amontillado.' I remember that someone got buried alive in the story. I wonder if this type of wine had some significance to the deceased."

Jake shook his head and picked up his hat. There was still one unpleasant job that had to be done. "Oh yeah, I'll call Dexter and let him know what's going on. We don't need for him to get on his high horse. We have agreed to keep all three jurisdictions informed and we'd better not leave the city out."

Dexter Paine was the chief of police in the city and neither Mark nor Jake could take too much of him at any one time. Since they were both professionals, they did not express their feelings about him, even between themselves, unless the situation became unbearable. Dexter, who was the not-very-bright son of a wealthy business man, had finally managed to graduate from a small college to which his father contributed handsomely. After several failed attempts in business, he had gone to work for the police force. Between his talent for ingratiating himself with those in charge and his father's pull with the local politicians, after ten years, Dexter had been appointed chief of police for the City. The power of the position, together with Dexter's personality, had proved to be an unfortunate combination.

"Thanks, Jake, see if you can keep him from getting involved.

The two of us should be able to handle this." Mark went outside, leaving the rest of the procedure in Jake's hands. The electronic chimes in the Chapel sounded two o'clock. Mr. Jefferson would have been appalled at the Gothic stone Chapel located so near the Rotunda. It had been built later in the 19th century with funds raised by good Christian ladies who wanted to compensate for Mr. Jefferson's lack of enthusiasm for organized religion.

The Chapel had been the site for many weddings and memorial services over the years, and in spite of Mr. Jefferson's admonitions regarding the separation of church and state, had come to be an integral part of the traditions at the University. Mark never heard the chimes without thinking of his own wedding, which had taken place in the Chapel years ago. He closed his mind to memories and concentrated on the work to be done.

Mark was just preparing to leave when his cell phone beeped. The operator told him that it was Ellen Randolph. Mark had known Ellen since he was a teenager, working summer jobs in maintenance on the Grounds. She had always been gracious to the summer employees, and he had sometimes stopped to talk with her when she was working late in the Rotunda. He had confided to her his hopes for joining the police force, and she had encouraged him to enter the program at the community college. She knew about his skills at horseback riding and showed genuine interest in his progress, and she always inquired about his parents as though she really cared.

"Mrs. Randolph, this is Mark. What can I do for you?"

He listened for several minutes, his expression becoming more concerned. "I'll be there as soon as I can turn this over to someone else. Let's make it 2:30."

CHAPTER FIVE

. . . With perhaps the exception of Yale, no other university can claim as many secret societies among its ranks . . . Secret societies may perhaps be the best extant link to the tradition-doused University . . . A certain unassailability of old ideas and ways exist in the rituals and behavior of these groups. Any self-respecting Virginia Gentleman would do his damndest to be asked to join.

University of Virginia Website

"The young man's name was Charles Allan, and he seemed to be both a very sensible and stable person." Ellen folded her hands on the desk to keep them from trembling. She had liked Charlie Allan. While the news of his death had upset her, she didn't want Mark to think she was being overly emotional in her account of what had transpired. "He first came to see me on January 29th because he had found something very unusual in his room and he wanted to ask me what I knew about it."

* * *

Charlie had barged into her office that day, with big flakes of wet snow clinging to his red hair and his glasses so fogged coming in from the cold that he could barely see where he was going. At first, Ellen had been annoyed at the abrupt entry, but his good-natured grin and sincere apology had changed her mind. She had invited him to sit and have a cup of tea with her. "Until your glasses clear up, sitting is the safest place for you," she had said, offering him a tissue.

Charlie, a graduate student in English, lived on the West range only a few doors from the Poe room. He had a fellowship for doctoral study while earning money as an instructor in the first-year courses. He also had a part-time job as a bartender at a pub on the Corner. The Corner was a row of shops and restaurants across from the Central Grounds of the University. When the student body of the University included only a few thousand white male students, the Corner shops had filled the students' needs for food, supplies and clothing. In the past 30 years, the University had grown to include 18,000 men and women of multi-races and many of these services were now provided on the Grounds of the University. Most of the shops on the Corner were now either bars or tourist traps full of overpriced mugs and shirts. Charlie worked in one of the pubs which, through the years, had changed from a poorly-lit student hangout of scarred dark wood and smoky mirrors to an upscale tourist attraction, complete with hanging plants and bright stained-glass windows.

Charlie had done his undergraduate work at Ohio State and was surprised when he won a fellowship to the prestigious University of Virginia's English department for work in American literature. He had been fascinated by gothic American writing, particularly the work of Edgar Allen Poe. A Midwesterner interested in studying Poe had intrigued the admissions' committee, and he had found himself in September housed in one of the rooms on the West range, living almost next door to the room in which Poe had spent his 10 months and one day as a student at the University.

One cool October night, Charlie had decided to build a fire in the fireplace in his room and had carried in a load of heavy logs from outside his door. Students bought the firewood from farmers driving through the Grounds and then kept the logs stacked outside their doors on the covered colonnade that ran the length of the range in front of the rooms. As he struggled to get a particularly heavy log into place, it had fallen out of his grasp and hit the corner of the fireplace hearth, dislodging one of the bricks. Attempting to replace the brick, he noticed that there was a hollow space beneath, and when he removed the brick, he discovered a very thin metal box wedged into the space. Someone had apparently scraped out a part of the mortar to accommodate the box, so the brick could be replaced without any noticeable effect from the outside. It was the contents of the box that had brought him to see Ellen Randolph, because he had been told that she would know something about it, if anyone did.

"It seems to be some kind of secret society, because there's a list of things that the members need to do as a part of their initiation." Charlie handed the box to Ellen and she removed the contents onto her desk.

"There is also a list of names in there. I found out from the registrar's office that they were graduate students here in the early 70's—in the English department. The woman in the registrar's office suggested you might know them."

"Indeed I do know them," Ellen replied, looking over the list. "My husband was the chairman of the English department at the time. All of these young men—I'm almost certain—were in his Poe seminar. He invited these young men to our home during the semester. So I got to know them, too."

"Do you have any idea where they are now?" Charlie's excitement at his discovery was evident, and Ellen smiled at his eagerness. He reminded her a little of her husband, Robert, because both were unlikely types to be English scholars. Her husband had been strong and athletic with a sort of boyish, blundering manner that endeared him to everyone.

"Well, let's see. One of them, Anthony Antonetti, is dead," she said, pointing to the first name on the list. "He was killed in an airplane accident soon after he graduated. Another, George Blake, is a judge up in Maine. I saw him a few years ago. He'd returned for a reunion, but his health was very poor. This one, Henry Dodson, he just disappeared one day before the end of the semester."

Ellen stared thoughtfully for a few minutes, recollecting the strange young man who had caused so many problems. "Apparently, he had been blackmailing some graduate student who had written a forged check. As you know, since the University Honor Code forbids stealing, and with the single sanction against lying, cheating, and stealing, that would probably have been grounds for immediate expulsion. The student went public with the matter and, even though he was expelled, he revealed this Henry Dodson to be a blackmailer. When Henry disappeared, everyone assumed that he had left because of the scandal. Since he had no family that anyone knew about, the matter was soon forgotten. Most people felt it was good riddance to a bad character."

"You mean he would have been expelled for this first offense of writing a forged check?" Charlie asked.

Ellen nodded. "My husband always thought the single sanction of expulsion was too severe. He advocated lesser penalties for many of these offenses—except for plagiarizing. He was adamant that students who deliberately took credit for the work of others should receive the most severe penalty."

"Then Henry Dodson would have been expelled as well, since what he had done in blackmailing other students would probably have been considered both lying and stealing." Charlie pointed to the paper listing the names and asked, "What about the rest of the men? Are any of them still around?" He was obviously concerned that all of the people on the list would turn out to be dead or missing, and he wanted to talk to someone about the secret society.

"The others live here in Charlottesville or nearby." Ellen smiled at Charlie's obvious relief. "Frank Gruver is a real estate developer in Albemarle County. His wife, Anne, is the daughter of the Episcopal priest in the Farmington church, Reverend George Evans. Their daughter, Sarah, is married to a professor in the physics department—a brilliant young man. John Grieco is a lawyer running for the state senate from this district. He is a fundamentalist Christian with very strong opinions."

"What about this last name, Ted Mitchell?" Charlie circled the name on the list with his finger. "Is he around?"

"He is very much around and you know him. His real name is Arnold Theodore Mitchell. Does that sound familiar?"

Charlie gaped in open-mouthed astonishment. "The dean of the college—Dean Mitchell—That's '*Ted*' Mitchell?"

"He could tell you more about this society than I can, and I'm certain that he would see you about it. All of the men were obviously interested in Poe, and they must have formed this secret society while living on the West range and writing their masters' theses. Secret societies, as you probably have gathered, are a very popular tradition at the University. I suspect that these young men decided that they would create one for themselves. Why don't you go and see Professor Mitchell?"

* * *

Ellen looked at Mark, who was listening to her account of her meeting with Charles Allan with rapt attention. "I only wish I had told him to go home and forget about the whole business," she sighed.

"This is very interesting, Ellen, but why do you think it indicates that the young man did not take his own life?"

"Mark, it is the initiation that I particularly want you to hear about. It so interested me that I asked Charlie the second time he came to see me if I could make a copy of it." She handed Mark a piece of paper from the drawer of her desk and watched as his expression changed from mild interest to astonishment. The steps of the initiation outlined on the paper were identical to the procedures taken by Charlie Allan in his supposed suicide.

The one to be initiated had to find the secret way into the room other than through the window or the door. This meant that the individual had to discover the entrance from the tunnels and through the trap door in the floor. In the room, the initiate would find a bottle of Amontillado wine. The initiate was to lie on the bed while drinking the wine and repeating the opening stanzas of "The Raven," but first he was to take the pen in the room and underline a line of poetry in the book on the table, "Quoth the Raven, 'Nevermore.'" A member of the society would come by outside the room at an agreed-upon hour and observe the individual through the plexiglass door, signaling his presence, when the coast was clear, with a flashlight beam flicked on and off three times. At that point, the one being initiated was to signal back with a flashlight, raise his glass in a toast and speak the words "Quoth the raven, 'Nevermore,' and then drink the glass of wine."

At this point, the initiate was to leave the room just as he had found it, including finding some way to return the chest to its original position as the trap door was lowered. Charlie had studied the room, Ellen told Mark, from outside the plexiglass door and determined that this could be done by balancing the chest against the wall and then sliding through the trap door and slowing releasing the chest into place from above. The person outside the door would check the room with the flashlight to make certain that all was in order. Then, the initiate was to come to the room, where Charlie had been living and where he had found Henry Dodson's metal box, in order to celebrate entrance into the society. He found out that his room was the one in which Henry Dodson had lived when he was a student.

"Charlie could have followed these directions as a way of taking his own life," Mark said.

"He could have, Mark, but I don't believe for a minute that he did." Ellen looked directly at Mark. "I am a pretty good judge of character, and Charlie was a person full of enthusiasm and vitality. He loved his studies, his work—and he was innately curious about everything. I bet it was his curiosity that got him killed." Ellen got up and went over to the window. In the reflection of the glass she imagined she could still see Charlie's grin and the way he tugged at the front of his hair. "Others know about this ritual. He even mentioned to me that one person had encouraged him to start the society again and had indicated a willingness to help him. Then Charlie smiled slyly and said this part was a big secret and 'I'm not supposed to tell anyone about it.' Someone used Charlie's curiosity to trick him into that room. I really think this was murder."

CHAPTER SIX

But, as in ethics, evil is a consequence of good, so, in fact, out of joy is sorrow born.

—Poe's "Berenice"

Mark returned to his office in the campus police station near the Grounds, after having checked the crime scene to make certain that the area had been cordoned off and University police assigned to a 24-hour guard to prevent vandalism. Most of the staff had gone home, when he spoke to the two officers who were still on duty in the front office. Mark made himself a cup of instant soup. It was on nights like this that he was almost relieved that no wife and family were waiting for him to come home for dinner.

Mark had been married for three years to his high school sweetheart, and he thought they had been reasonably happy. One day he came home to find a note saying that she was leaving and would be in touch. Their bank account had been emptied, and she had taken their one good car. Months later, he received divorce papers in the mail, which he signed. Last year, a letter from her arrived saying that she was remarried and working on a college degree. She also sent Mark a check for half the amount she had removed from the account and half the book value of the car she had taken. There was no explanation in the letter for why she had left or any acknowledgment of her feelings for him. She wished him well and thanked him for having saved her from her family. He thought of writing and asking her what had gone wrong, but he never did, and now he never thought about writing—but he did think about her.

Mark realized that he had never known his wife. A cheerleader when he played basketball, she had been cute and a good dancer.

He was proud to be with her and to protect her from an abusive home situation. They got married after graduation, and she had seemed content to be a housewife and to fit into life in Charlottesville—until the day she walked away from him. It was only after she was gone that he realized how much he needed her. For weeks, he could not stay in the house. He expected her to come through the door or to sit down with him at the table. He realized they had seldom talked with each other. He had talked, and she had listened. Mark buried himself in his work and his dedication had been rewarded. Now he was the chief, and he lived alone in the spartan apartment he rented after he sold his house. He did not think about the loneliness anymore. It was just part of his life, like his work.

He sat down in the battered swivel chair in his office and leaned his elbows on the equally battered desk to think over his conversation with Ellen. He trusted her judgement, and there *was* a puzzling set of coincidences between the secret society and Charlie's strange death. He looked over the coroner's reports and found nothing that he had not expected. The young man had died of strychnine and a number of sleeping pills in the wine. The sleeping pills would have prevented him from prolonged suffering. There was no evidence that he had been struck, strangled, or smothered, and his entry into the room was apparently voluntary. His fingerprints were found on the book, the table, the pen and the flashlight, and there was no evidence that the area had been wiped clean of prints.

Still, it was not his experience that a student would take his life in such a dramatic way. The death of a person committing suicide was usually as dreary and forlorn as their life had become. If someone had the energy and imagination to create a dramatic suicide, the chances are that the person would have the energy to keep on living and try to solve their problems. In addition, this man did not sound like the dramatic and tortured type of personality who would go to such extremes.

He was reading the information in the file when the vice chancellor of the University, Bowman Ward, came into his office and carefully pulled the door closed in a very deliberate gesture.

Bowman had been the vice chancellor for 23 years. He was an able administrator who had amassed considerable authority. As university chancellors had come and gone during his tenure, he was the one person to maintain continuous power. Vigorous and handsome, he regularly worked out at the country club and the athletic club.

Bowman had been married and divorced long ago, and his only daughter lived in California. It was common wisdom that he was wed to his work. He worked long hours and was usually the first to arrive and last to leave his office on the Lawn. He had inherited wealth and was a member of the Virginia aristocracy—a first family. It was his horse farm on which Mark's father was the trainer. Many thought that Bowman would eventually become chancellor of the University, but he knew that he could never play the games a chancellor must play. He was too quick to anger and to express his opinions bluntly. His role was to be the power behind the throne, and he relished that power.

"I understand you investigated the suicide on the Grounds this morning, Mark."

"Yes, sir, it seems to be a suicide, but there are things about it that just don't seem right."

"Like what things?"

Bowman's voice had that low, calm quality that often meant trouble was brewing. Mark was feeling uneasy. "Well, for instance, it was very dramatic for a suicide. Everything was staged as if for a production. Ellen Randolph told me that . . ."

"What has Ellen Randolph got to do with this?" The chancellor's voice was almost hostile.

"She called me and I went to see her. She knew the victim. She also knew that he had found some information regarding a secret society in his room, and the initiation rites were identical to the way in which this suicide, or whatever it was, was staged."

"And why do you say 'whatever it was,' Mark? Do you have any doubts?" Bowman was looking at him with a kind of grim disapproval.

"Ellen didn't think that this young man was the type of person to commit suicide."

"And when did Ellen Randolph become an expert on the psychology of suicidal behavior?"

"I trust her judgement, Bowman, but that's not the only thing. The whole scene just didn't feel right to me."

"Well, we have Ellen Randolph's intuition and your feelings. Hardly a scientific combination." The vice chancellor leaned across the desk to emphasize his words. "You know we can expect student suicides around this time of the year, and we have an agreement with the press not to publicize these tragic events because of the possibility of copy-cat behavior by other students. We don't want this event to become 'newsworthy.' The University does not need any more bad publicity, after all that has been happening to the athletic teams and that absurd situation at the hospital."

"I can't run this department out of fear of the press, Bowman," Mark replied quietly.

The older man sighed and sat down facing Mark. "I don't expect you to, and I regret if I came across too harshly on this, Mark. It is just that we have been having a lot of bad press lately and I'm the one that feels the heat on these matters. Please don't waste any more time on this, Mark. A despondent student commits suicide at the end of the semester. It happens frequently. This one just chose a somewhat different way to go about it. Please help me keep all of this out of the media. The press could have a field day with this if they get started. On top of that, graduation is in a few days and parents will be all over the Grounds. We don't need yellow tape and police surveillance teams at the Poe room to attract their attention."

Mark understood what Bowman was saying. The national press had been running front page stories about the behavior of some of the athletes at the University and of two newborn babies sent home from the hospital with the wrong parents. Mark knew that Bowman was feeling the pressure from the Board of Regents and the chancellor to control the flood of negative publicity. "All right, Bowman. There really doesn't seem to be any Grounds for an investigation. I'll close the books on this one as quickly and quietly as possible, and we will restore the Poe room to its normal appearance before graduation." After Bowman left, Mark sat for several minutes staring at the faded green carpet on the office floor. He didn't feel right about his decision. Something about this situation was unsettling, and Ellen's information made it even more so. He asked himself if he was giving in because Bowman was a powerful man at the University, and he was an employee of that same University. Well, he had made a decision, and he would stick to it. He would call Jake and tell him what had occurred. He was certain that Jake would go along with his decision.

The next morning, Mark called Ellen Randolph.

"I won't be keeping that appointment, Ellen, to discuss any further possibilities. You and I really don't have anything to go on except for our hunches. You know how sensitive the University is about keeping suicides out of the papers. Bowman Ward was here, and he has asked me to get this investigation over with as soon as possible. I think we'd better wrap up this case and let the University go about the business of graduation."

"But, Mark, I—" Ellen started to speak, but Mark interrupted her.

"There is nothing I can do about it, Ellen," he replied, more gruffly than he had intended. "My hands are tied on this one. I appreciate that you liked this young man, but there is nothing to indicate this is anything but an unusual suicide. His mother has arrived to take his body home. We just have no reason to continue our investigation. She's a widow. Charlie was her only child. She wants to go home as soon as possible. We are going to have to let this one go."

Ellen hung up the phone. She felt sorrow for Charlie's mother and did not want to add to her grief. She knew that the University feared publicity on suicides because other students could be encouraged to take the same way out of their problems. But she also knew that this case was different. Now, she would not have the opportunity to discuss with Mark one other item that had been in the box which she had remembered after he had left her office. Perhaps if Mark could not investigate this matter, she could quietly ask some questions on her own.

Mark sat in his office, holding the receiver in his hands for several minutes before replacing it. He did not like what he had just done. There was something about Ellen that had always made him want to be at his best and to make her respect him. Since he was a kid hanging around her office during his breaks in the summer, he had admired her. A smile or a compliment from Ellen meant a great deal to him then, and he found that it still did. Hearing the disappointment in her voice made him aware he had compromised himself in some way, and he did not like the feeling. He felt that there was more to this than a simple suicide, and yet there was no reason for him to pursue it any further. What Bowman had said made sense. He could not just go on his feelings. As he turned out the light, he thought that his feelings had gotten him into trouble in the past, and perhaps it was just as well that he keep them tightly under wraps.

CHAPTER SEVEN

Thou wast all that to me, love
For which my soul did pine—
—Poe's "To One in Paradise"

"Good morning, are you awake in there?" Fannie's warm voice floated up from the patio as she made her way into the kitchen. Ellen finished brushing her silver hair, which was still full and fell in waves to her shoulders when she set it free from the pins that held it in place.

"I'm coming, just give me one minute," she called, as she rolled her hair expertly into a french twist and patted any stray wisps into place. It had been so many years since Robert had kissed the nape of her neck as she brushed her hair, yet she still thought of that caress and yearned for the warmth of that close relationship. She smiled at her image in the glass and thought how amused her young friends would be if they knew she still harbored such feelings about a kiss on the neck.

She went down the stairs of the little town house she rented near the historic downtown area of Charlottesville to greet her friend. Most Saturday mornings, Fannie arrived with fresh bread or pastry and Ellen had the coffee and juice ready. They visited with each other for an hour or two, sharing the week's events and laughing over some of the experiences of their week that they did not care to share with anyone else.

Ellen poured the coffee as she listened to an account of Fannie's weekly visit at the judge's house.

"I was in the kitchen washin' up the mess after their big party and in comes 'hizzoner' in his under drawers—bony legs and all. He just looks through me like I wasn't even there and proceeds to pour himself a cup of coffee. It was all I could do to keep from staring at those bony knees, but I concentrated on the dishes till he ambled back upstairs without saying a word to me."

"That man has the manners of a goat," Ellen laughed, "and knees like one too, I gather."

Fannie and Ellen had been friends for over twenty-five years and each of them valued these mornings together as a special part of the week. Once, long ago, Fannie had cleaned Ellen's house, just as she cleaned others, and they had been polite and friendly as mistress and maid. Ellen had paid Fannie an adequate, but not a generous, wage and, like others, neglected to make any social security payments. She offered Fannie her used clothes before they went to the Salvation Army and sometimes Fannie accepted them. Ellen had known very little about Fannie other than the fact she was competent, honest, and reliable.

Then, one morning, Ellen Randolph's comfortable world ended. The car in which her husband and daughter were driving was struck by a tractor trailer and both were killed instantly. Ellen was told just as she was about to leave her lovely pavilion on the Lawn. The scene that bright fall day the instant she heard the news was etched in her memory—two students moving across the Lawn, a squirrel about to dash up a tree, lovers holding hands in an archway, a workman repairing a sidewalk. However, for the month following that moment, all other memories were lost. She moved through the double funeral in a daze and each morning she awoke more removed from reality.

Then came a morning when Ellen could not get dressed. She simply lay in the bed and hoped to die. Friends came and brought food and tried to talk to her, but she stared at the wall. Finally, the friends stopped trying to communicate, but Ellen didn't notice. The Episcopal priest, Reverend Evans, came and urged her to get up and become a part of God's world again. Her voice full of the anger she felt toward God and his messenger, she asked him to leave her house.

Some time went by before Ellen realized that there was a presence in the house, moving about and straightening up, not saying anything. Warm milk would appear on the night table, a clean gown was lying across the bed, and the sheets were changed while she was in the bathroom.

For several days she did not care to know who was there, but little by little she began to come back to herself. One morning, she got out of bed, put on her robe and went looking for the mysterious presence. She found Fannie Groomes. The kitchen was clean and scrambled eggs and toast were on the table.

"I thought maybe you would feel like a little breakfast this morning," was all Fannie had said, as she poured Ellen a cup of strong, hot coffee.

Ellen found to her amazement that she was hungry and the eggs and toast were delicious. She said nothing and Fannie said nothing. When she was finished, she murmured only a "thank you" and went back to her room. In the evening, she heard Fannie in the kitchen again and smelled the delicious aroma of fresh bread. This time, the two of them spoke a few words, but mostly Fannie placed some food before her and then quietly left.

Almost a week went by with this pattern of interaction, as Ellen gradually regained her strength, before she and Fannie had a real conversation. It was Ellen who opened the communication by asking quietly, "Why are you doing this, Fannie? Has someone sent you here?"

"No one sent me," Fannie replied. She hung the dishcloth on the hook over the sink and sat down across from Ellen at the table. She reached her dark hand across the table and placed it on Ellen's. "I came because I know how you feel. My husband was killed in Korea, leaving me with a little boy to raise. My son was my whole life, and what a child he was—strong and smart, a good student and a star athlete. He was going places. Then, one day, he was shot down in Richmond by a gang who mistook him for someone else. My world just ended. I couldn't talk to anyone or even stand to be in the same room with anyone else. I almost hit the preacher when he came to my house, too."

For the first time in weeks, Ellen felt a smile crack her frozen features. "I don't remember what I said to him, but I think I was pretty rude to Reverend Evans."

"Word has it that you almost threw a vase of flowers at him," Fannie chuckled. "Your friends don't know why you are acting so strangely towards them, but I know. I couldn't stand to have anyone around me, particularly those wanting to talk and console. I just needed to be alone. Folks behave in different ways to tragedy. I could tell that you and I were alike."

Ellen planned to repay Fannie for her time and effort, but a few weeks after she began to come back to life she had another blow. Her husband, who had handled all of the business in the family, had speculated in local bonds and all of their savings had been lost. He had some life insurance through the University, but most of that went to pay off her debts. They had sold their home when they moved onto the University Grounds, and all of the money from the sale of the house had been lost in the investments. She was essentially penniless and soon to be homeless, since the pavilion would be assigned to another faculty member.

"Fannie, I can't pay you for any more of your help, and I'll have to owe you for some of your time. I just don't know what I would have done without you, but I'm out of money." Ellen still had difficulty believing that her life had altered so dramatically.

"You don't owe me for anything. I came because I wanted—no—I *needed*, to come. This has helped to heal some of my pain, too, just being able to help you."

"Fannie, I feel like you are my closest friend right now. Is it possible that we could continue to visit with each other?"

That was the way their friendship had begun and it had not faltered over the years.

* * *

Ellen poured each of them another cup of coffee and nibbled at a corner of one of the muffins. "I understand that the University is concerned about copy-cat suicides and bad publicity, but Bowman Ward should not let that stand in the way of getting to the truth. Ignoring a problem like the disappearance of a student, for instance, only leads to more problems."

"You know," Fannie stirred her coffee thoughtfully, after putting in three teaspoons of sugar and ignoring Ellen's disapproving frown, "I remember the morning that young man, the blackmailer, disappeared from the University—the one the dead boy was asking you about. I was cleaning at the Evans house that morning, and Bowman Ward came over all in a rush. He and Reverend Evans were shut up in the study for hours."

Ellen thought back over the years to recall Bowman's responsibilities at the University. "Bowman was an assistant to the chancellor then, and I suppose he was given the job of keeping the lid on negative publicity, just as he is today."

"I was about to vacuum the living room, and Mrs. Evans asked me to concentrate on the kitchen and the bedrooms because they had important business to discuss and didn't want to be disturbed. Miss Anne was upstairs and, when I caught a glimpse of her, her face was swollen from crying. That was a long time ago, but I've wondered about it many times. She knew the boy who had gone missing, because I saw him at the house with her and some other young people one time. I just figured it all had something to do with his disappearance."

"That was another case that didn't get very much investigation," Ellen replied thoughtfully. The student who disappeared, Henry Dodson, was in disgrace and about to be expelled after the blackmailing incident. He did not have any family except an elderly grandmother who was unable to travel. After a few weeks, he just seemed to be forgotten as though he had never existed." Fannie walked over and looked out at the flowers growing on the little patio—pink and white geraniums in pots and wisteria climbing the brick wall. "Anne was such a sweet, bubbly little thing when she was young. She got married soon after that morning to the Gruver boy, and she and her husband moved away for several years. When she came back, she sure was the serious matron lady."

Ellen smiled because Anne certainly did everything possible to look matronly. "Bowman Ward may be able to tell Mark what to do, but he can't order me around. I plan to look into this a little further."

"Just keep in mind," Fannie said, "your friend, Charlie, was just curious about this situation, too. He ended up dead! You best watch out for yourself."

CHAPTER EIGHT

Students have treated the tunnels as an underground adventure over the years . . .

"Inside UVa," May 2, 1997

Ellen had not been in Ted Mitchell's study in many years. He and his wife, Rebecca, lived in the pavilion next to the one in which she had lived with her husband and daughter so many years ago.

When she had called Ted for an appointment, he had insisted on meeting her in his home. His wife, Rebecca, was away, he had told her, but Fannie's sister, Etta Mae Toliver, was there to make them some tea. Etta Mae had opened the door for her and shown her into the study. "You make yourself comfortable and I'll go and let him know you are here."

Ellen walked around the comfortable room, savoring the feeling of being in the study of a serious scholar again. Some of the books looked familiar, and she seemed to remember giving many of Robert's books to Ted after the accident. She began to scan the shelves more carefully to see if she recognized any of the titles. At the end of one of the shelves, she noticed Ted's doctoral dissertation and next to it his master's thesis on Poe's tragic heroines. She remembered that Robert had thought very highly of Ted's writing and research and had described him as a leading Poe scholar. As she reached to lift the thesis from the shelf, Ted appeared in the doorway and Ellen pulled back her hand.

"I am so pleased to see you again, Ellen." Ted was not a handsome man, but he was always elegantly dressed and meticulously groomed. His students referred to him in private as "dapper Dan." He had a full head of wavy hair, and there were those who insisted that it must be a toupee. If it was, Ellen thought, it was most believable.

"Rebecca will be so sorry to have missed you."

Ellen thought to herself that Ted's arrogant and cool wife would not in the least have missed seeing her. According to Fannie, who got her information from Etta Mae, Ted and Rebecca had a marriage in name only. Rebecca traveled much of the time, but returned to Charlottesville in the fall to entertain and to be a part of the local social scene. Ted had a long and very discreet "friendship" with a wealthy widow. Everyone pretended that Ted and Rebecca were a loving couple and almost everyone knew otherwise.

Ellen was saved from having to make some reply regarding Rebecca's sorrow at having missed her by the entry of Etta, bearing a tea service on a tray and some biscuits.

"Ah, Etta, thank you very much. I hope that we did not inconvenience you."

"No, sir, I am jist pleased to fix this for you. Is there any thing else I can git for you folks?" Etta bobbed, in what was almost a curtsy.

Etta Mae glanced at the astonished Ellen, as she placed the tray on the table, and gave her a slight wink. The dialect was a sham. Ellen knew that Etta Mae spoke standard English as well as Fannie. The tall, attractive black woman was Fannie's youngest sister. She had been married and lived for several years in Richmond, where her husband was a fireman. When the marriage had broken up, Etta Mae came back to live near Fannie in the family home. She was smart and had a beautiful singing voice, but she also had two children to support. Cleaning houses was about all she really knew how to do, except "to sing her head off in church," as she had told Ellen. "Most of the time it isn't too bad. People don't expect slave labor, like they once did. They know how hard it is to find reliable help, but I have to mind my tongue and my manners sometimes."

Once, Fannie had explained to Ellen that she and Etta May put the people they worked for into three general categories. The first group was the weasels—mean-spirited types like the judge, who were rude and pretended that the "help" were not even in the room. Then there were the tolerables—patronizing, overly solicitous types like Ted, who pretended concern and interest and then forgot to write a check. Etta Mae was providing the stereotype that Ted already had in his head of the subservient "colored" maid. The third group, the primes, treated those who worked for them as professionals. They gave clear instructions, paid well, gave a day or two of paid vacation every year, and made social security payments on time.

Ellen thought that she had probably been more like Ted, in the tolerable category, years ago, when she had lived on the Lawn and Fannie had been her maid, rather than a friend. She had had shallow attitudes about race and working class people in general, having never worked and having inherited the easy prejudice of privileged Virginians. It had taken tragedy and years of experience for Ellen to understand the person she had been and to appreciate the person she had become.

"The young man who committed suicide came to see me after you gave him my name." Ted poured the tea competently, remembering that she took lemon. "I liked him very much and told him everything I could remember about our secret society—which wasn't too much, I'm afraid."

"You know that he followed the procedures of the initiation in taking his life," Ellen said, looking closely at Ted's reaction.

"That was so strange to me," Ted replied. "He just didn't seem like the type of person to commit suicide."

"I don't think so either, Ted." The concern was obvious in Ellen's voice and Ted looked at her closely. "I just don't believe that he would have committed suicide and certainly not in this manner."

"But don't the police feel certain that is what happened? Bowman Ward assured me that they were closing the case and that they had enough evidence to support a ruling of suicide."

"Yes, that's what I have been told." Ellen decided suddenly not to indicate the level of her concern to Ted. "I just thought that he was a very pleasant young man and deserved to have some interest shown in his life." For the first time, Ellen had a strange sensation that she was in this by herself and that perhaps no one, other than Fannie, could be trusted with her most serious doubts.

"That must have been a very interesting society that you men were a part of." Ellen smiled, as though she were changing the subject. "How did you ever come to think of it?"

"It was really Henry Dodson's idea. We had no idea at the time that he was such an unpleasant character. He seemed very charming." Ted got up and began to pace around the room, obviously disturbed. "I really liked Henry at first. I can't believe what a poor judge of character I was. I believe he would have tried to blackmail everyone in the society if he had not skipped out after one of his victims finally turned him in."

"How did he find out all the things he used against people?"

"He was very clever. He listened carefully to conversations. He encouraged people to talk to him and pretended to be a concerned listener. I'm sure that he also looked through papers when he had an opportunity, since we all came and went into each others rooms."

"Did he actually try to blackmail any of the members of the society?"

"It came out later that he had. He found out that Tony Antonetti, God rest his soul, was not a legal citizen. He was here on an extended green card, having lived with his grandmother for several years. As an alien, he was not supposed to have a fellowship. And then there was George Blake. As a young teenager, he had a felony offense on his record, having once been convicted of stealing a car. The case was appealed due to extenuating circumstances and George was given a reprimand and then released. However, he hadn't told the admissions committee, and Henry threatened to make the incident public. I suppose George has been relieved many times over the years, as he was appointed to higher positions on the bench, that his record never became public."

"What about those of you who are still in the Charlottesville area—Frank Gruver, John Grieco and you—were any of you ever threatened?" Ellen tried to mask her curiosity and appear to be only mildly interested, but Ted was so wrapped up in his own memories of that time that he didn't seem concerned about her questions.

"Not to my knowledge. But I 'm certain that he would have gotten around to us before he was through. It's so hard for me to believe that a person we all liked, a person who was our friend, could have fooled us so completely."

Ted went over to the bookshelf and took down a photo album. "Look at all of us in those days," he said, opening the album and indicating a photo to Ellen. "It's hard to imagine that there could have been something so terribly wrong with Henry."

Ellen looked closely at the photograph of the smiling young faces. The students were gathered on the colonnade in front of one of the rooms on the West range. Chairs had been pulled out onto the covered walkway and a table held the remains of a party, with wine bottles sitting on the ground. Several young women were also included in the group. An attractive brunette was sitting in Ted's lap, another young woman was leaning against the doorway, and a third was standing with her arm around Henry Dodson. Ellen studied the face of this young woman carefully and was certain that it was Anne Gruver, then Anne Evans.

"Who is that attractive girl in your lap, Ted?" Ellen asked, not really caring, but not wanting to appear overly interested in the young woman with Henry.

"I don't even remember. I think she was a nursing student. They were about the only women on the Grounds in those days, except for the ones in the school of education. We almost got into big trouble one night by going through the tunnels and up into the nursing dorm. We got out just before the police arrived. After that, the University closed off some of the tunnels to keep students out of particular areas. I can't believe that I was ever young enough and foolish enough to think of such pranks. We all traveled around in the tunnels in those days. For some reason we thought that it was great fun. I think most of them are locked now."

"This young woman next to Henry looks like Anne Gruver."

"Yes, I seem to remember that Anne went with Henry for a while before she got interested in Frank. She was in her first year at Sweetbriar—just a girl, really. I think they met at the church where her father is the rector. Lucky for her that nothing serious developed between them."

Ellen looked at the picture again and noted that Anne was gazing at Henry with an expression on her face that seemed to be very serious indeed, but she said nothing about her observation to Ted.

Ellen left Ted's house that afternoon with many more questions than answers—and a deepening sense of uneasiness.

CHAPTER NINE

But our love it was stronger by far than the love
Of those who were older than we.

—*Poe's "Annabelle Lee"*

Ellen had not intended to talk to Anne Gruver so soon, but it seemed that fate, or rather their faith, put them together. Anne called her the next day to schedule a meeting regarding Ellen's pledge to the Episcopal church. Anne was a member of the budget committee and Ellen was on her list of members to be visited regarding her pledge. For once, Ellen was delighted because she very much wanted to speak to Anne about the group in the photo.

Two evenings later, Anne was sitting in Ellen's small, but beautifully furnished, living room. She was an attractive, matronly woman who wore little makeup and had her hair cut in a severely short style. She was dressed, as usual, in a plain and rather unbecoming skirt and blouse and flat, practical shoes. Ellen thought that in spite of her lack of attention to style, Anne was still very attractive and her face had a sweetness and openness that could not be disguised.

Anne asked about some of the antiques in Ellen's living room, particularly about a chest that had belonged to Ellen's mother. She had managed to keep a few very special pieces when she sold her antiques, and this was a particularly fine chest from the Federal period.

"You know, Ellen, many people still remember how beautifully you decorated your home on the Lawn."

"That was a very long time ago," Ellen smiled. "My mother had given me many antiques that were perfect in the pavilion."

"You have made a fine life for yourself, Ellen. I admire you very much." Anne spoke directly and without any affectation, and Ellen thought again how much she liked this woman.

"When you went to work for the University, no one really thought that a woman would make that much difference. I remember the other women talking about what an impossible task it would be for you, but you showed them all." Anne's face warmed with a smile.

"I didn't have much choice, Anne. I needed to earn a living, and when the chancellor offered me the opportunity, I had to take it. To tell you the truth, I wasn't certain that I could do it, either." Ellen laughed as she thought of the mistakes she had made and of the slow process of learning to be assertive and give directions to others—particularly to men. Gradually, she discovered that leadership was a pleasure and a privilege—and that she was good at it.

Ellen had grown up in Charlottesville in a lovely Georgian home on Park Street, just off the historic Courthouse Square and not far from the townhouse where she was now living. Her father was a lawyer who loved walking to Court Square, where his office was located in one of the 18th-century buildings facing the historic Jefferson-designed Courthouse. Her mother was a lovely, talented woman who played the piano, painted in water colors, and raised her daughter, who had been a surprise late in life. This she did, of course, with the help of several loyal servants. It had never occurred to Ellen that she would ever be expected to work for a living. She was a Lee who had married a Randolph, and that should have been a guarantee for life.

It should have been some kind of warning to her when her father and mother died within a few years of each other and left almost no estate. The house on Park Street was sold to pay off the debts, and Robert had teased her that he had thought he was marrying an heiress, not a poor homeless waif. Looking back, however, Ellen was convinced that he had taken chances with their finances because he thought that Ellen would have a secure inheritance. Ellen served tea and, after the obligatory discussion regarding her pledge to the church, Ellen brought up the subject of the death of the young man in the Poe room. "I know that Frank was a part of the secret group in which Charlie became so interested."

"We were all friends. The men had formed this secret society and we thought it was great fun. Who would have guessed how it would turn out." Anne's voice was suddenly full of sadness.

"I don't think Charlie killed himself, Anne. I think he was murdered, perhaps because of something he found out about the society."

Anne looked at Ellen for several moments without answering and then she took a deep breath and settled herself in the chair. "Ellen, I have a confession to make. I took this opportunity as a member of the budget committee for the purpose of visiting with you. I know you're interested in what happened because you liked the young man, uh Charlie, who was found in the Poe room, and I have my own reasons to be interested also. I think that you should know the facts. I trust you and I don't believe that you would ever indulge in gossip or repeat what I am about to tell you." Anne smiled, but Ellen could tell she was nervous.

"I've no intention of any idle gossip, Anne," Ellen spoke very seriously. "If Charlie did not take his own life, however, I don't know what that will mean. I can't promise to keep secret something that might have a bearing on a murder."

"I trust you Ellen. Just promise to talk with me before you say anything to anyone else." Anne searched Ellen's face for assurance and received it from an outstretched hand and warm smile. "Both my daughter, Sarah, and I are very anxious to know more. You see, Sarah has been looking for her biological father for several years."

As Ellen listened in astonishment, Anne told her that Sarah was not the daughter of Frank Gruver.

"Sarah's father was Henry Dodson. After Henry's disappearance, I married Frank, and we went away to live for several years. Sarah was born just a few months after our marriage. When we returned to town with Sarah and our two boys, everyone had forgotten about my relationship with Henry. Actually, Ellen, I'm not even sure what that relationship was. I was totally captivated by Henry's charm and wit. I was only nineteen. When he found out that I was pregnant, his reaction was very strange. He became distant when we were together. Then he disappeared before I was able to find out what was wrong."

Ellen poured more tea into their cups. "Did you have any idea what had become of him? Did he leave a note or anything?"

"There was nothing, Ellen. He just vanished and everything he owned was gone from his room. When the story of his blackmailing attempts was made public, I assumed, like others, he had just run away to escape punishment."

Anne accepted a cup of tea that Ellen had poured from the tea service on the table between them and carefully stirred sugar into the cup. "When Sarah was sixteen, I told her the truth about her father against Frank's wishes. I felt that Sarah had a right to know about her parentage. When we discussed it, Sarah told me that she had thought for some time that there was some part of her life that was missing."

"You said that Sarah has been trying to find Henry Dodson. Has she had any success?"

"Henry seems to have totally disappeared," Anne continued. "Frank paid for a private investigator to help her—in spite of his own feelings. But no trace was found. Frank has always been wonderful to me and to Sarah. He is a very good man, but I don't know if he will ever truly understand how much we both love him."

"What about Sarah's husband? Does he know the whole story?"

"Sarah told him before they were married, and he has also helped her in the search for her father. I hope that nothing comes out in all this that will hurt those two people." Anne's composure broke for the first time and her face crumpled in distress. Ellen moved closer to her and took her hand.

"Whatever happens, Anne, you have a strong family, and you and Sarah certainly care deeply about each other."

"Frank and I have worked hard to make a good home for Sarah and our boys." Anne took a handkerchief from her purse and wiped away the tears. Ellen could see that it was taking a great effort for Anne to regain control of herself. "What started out as a painful and uncertain relationship has proved to be a wonderful marriage. But, you know, the shadows of the past still linger in the dark corners. When there are secrets in a marriage, there are problems—always having to remember there are things that must not be told, catching yourself just in time before confiding in a friend. I hope that someday we can be open about our lives. But for right now I just don't want anyone else to get hurt."

"For your sake, Anne, when the time comes for the truth to be told, I hope it comes from you and from no one else. Right now, we don't know for sure that Charlie did not take his own life. It is only my suspicion, and frankly no one else seems to share my concern."

CHAPTER TEN

. . . Our talk had been serious and sober,
But our thoughts they were palsied and sere—
—Poe's "Ulalume"

Ellen was mistaken about no one else being concerned. The next evening she had a visit from Reverend Evans, Anne's father, and it was not about her pledge to his church. He made it clear to Ellen that he thought her interference in the matter should stop.

"What happened years ago has no bearing on this young man's unfortunate death. Why in the world would you want to stir up trouble, Ellen? Do you have nothing better to do with your time?"

Ellen looked closely at the imposing man sitting in her living room, his face barely concealing his anger. He was tall and gaunt, with thick eyebrows. When he stood in the pulpit in his robes, Ellen thought about the prophet Elijah. He had a powerful speaking voice, which could be very compelling; but Ellen also found it to be often haughty and unyielding. Ellen knew that he was extremely conservative in his views and was opposed to the ordination of women and homosexuals in the church. Ellen thought how much she loved the church in which she had grown up, where her great-grandfather had been a founding member, and how uncertain she had always felt about Reverend Evans as her minister.

Ellen wondered what could possibly cause this man to be so upset about an event that had occurred many years ago. Surely, the fact that Henry Dodson was the father of Anne's child could not possibly cause that much concern over thirty years later, especially since all of the people directly involved already knew about the situation; and Anne had been willing, even eager, to find out more about Charlie's death.

"Did Anne ask you to come here and persuade me to mind my own business?" Ellen tried to keep the anger out of her voice.

"Of course not. She is as stubborn and foolish as you. She doesn't seem to realize how unnecessary it is to bring up a lot of old business that is better forgotten. When she told me that she had confided everything to you, I was aghast."

"If Anne does not think it is better forgotten, then why are you so concerned? Anne is not a child, and she can certainly make her own decisions." Ellen's anger began to change to pity for the distraught man before her.

"Anne is a foolish woman. She has never fully understood the damage this information could cause if it should become public."

"I am afraid that the damage may already have been done. Henry Dodson disappeared years ago, and no one was anxious to find out what happened to him. Charlie comes along asking questions about the past and now he is dead, and too many people seem to be satisfied to forget the whole matter. Well, I am not one of those people, and I would hardly call Anne 'a foolish woman.'"

Reverend Evans tensed—and then suddenly slumped in his chair. He sat without speaking for several minutes, his hands over his eyes, and then he looked at Ellen with an intensity that frightened her more than his anger.

"I have to trust you, Ellen, just as Anne has trusted you with her secret, but even Anne does not know what I am about to tell you." Reverend Evans was very pale and his hands clutched at the sides of the chair. "Henry Dodson was blackmailing me. He threatened to abandon Anne and claim that he was not the father of her baby if I did not pay him a large sum of money. The only person who knows this is Bowman Ward. After Henry disappeared, Bowman advised me to say nothing about the blackmailing or Anne's pregnancy, but just to let the whole matter fade away, since she was going to marry Frank Gruver. That is what happened until this young man's unfortunate death—by his own hand—and your unnecessary questions." Reverend Evan's eyes began to flash once again with anger.

"But what about Frank?" Ellen asked, choosing to ignore his

comment. "Surely, he was ready to marry Anne. How would Henry Dodson have been able to carry out his threat to abandon Anne if Frank was there waiting to marry her?"

"I don't think Henry knew how Frank felt about Anne. Perhaps even Frank did not know for sure. I invited Frank to my office, and I begged him to marry my daughter. I offered to pay his way through graduate school. That is when I found out that Frank had been in love with Anne for months, but had said nothing to anyone. He refused my offer to pay his way through school and went to work in real estate." For a moment, it seemed that Reverend Evans was going to ask her for help. But, immediately, his face became stern and prideful. "Ellen, I don't want you to tell Anne about this. She might not understand—even today."

"If it is possible, I will not tell anyone," Ellen assured him. "I respect Anne very much, and I would never wish to see her hurt. If we can keep this secret about Henry Dodson, I will be very relieved. But, don't underestimate your daughter. She is a very strong woman and so is your granddaughter."

After Reverend Evans left, Ellen sat for a long time, with her hands folded in her lap, and thought about her conversations with Anne and her father. After a few minutes, she stood up and turned off the lights.

"Oh what a tangled web we weave when first we practice to deceive," she murmured to herself. The poet was certainly right about deception tangling people's lives and the lives of their children. She didn't want anyone to be hurt, but she also felt an obligation to Charlie and to the truth.

CHAPTER ELEVEN

Underneath the University of Virginia lies a vast, dusty, network of steam tunnels . . . infernal, arid, endlessly labyrinthine.
www.people.virginia.edu

On Saturday morning, Ellen and Fannie were back at the kitchen table sharing some fresh bagels with cream cheese and a pot of coffee.

"I hate that yuppie bagel place," Fannie snorted. "All those health food nuts standing in line for bagels because they don't have any fat in them and then ordering bagel sandwiches filled with fried eggs and bacon. How dumb can you get! But I do like these warm bagels, and I just didn't have time to bake this morning."

Fannie was all curves where Ellen was angles. She was a short, plump woman but carried herself with great dignity. In her Saturday outfit of a bright turban and African robe, which she had made with other women from her church, Ellen thought she looked like a queen, but when she shared this observation with Fannie, the reply was, "Well, this queen could sure use a day off from scrubbing toilets. You know where I might find some of my loyal and obedient subjects that would like that job?"

Ellen did not share the information she had been given by Anne and her father with Fannie, but she did confide her frustration about what had happened to Henry Dodson. "He just seems to have dropped off the earth. Ted told me that no one has seen or heard from him since the day he disappeared. He did show me pictures of the society taken with some young women. Besides Anne, there were two nursing students. Nursing and education were essentially the only two schools in which women were enrolled then."

Fannie shook her head and reached for another bagel. "Remember how ugly it was around here when the women arrived? It was worse than when the black students came in the 60's. Here is this state-supported university, and they thought that first blacks and then women should be kept out. No wonder we still have so many problems. That reminds me. I overheard Mrs. Larsen talking on the phone about how upset she was just thinking that dear Mr. Jefferson would be accused of 'having relations' with a slave. I almost went in and banged her on the head with the broom. How about being upset that 'dear Mr. Jefferson' had slaves in the first place." Fannie jabbed the bagel with the butter knife. "Besides, from what I have observed around here, there isn't anything too unusual about a gentleman sleeping with his sister-in-law. His slave, Sally Hemmings, and Jefferson's wife had the same daddy."

"I am glad you restrained yourself with that broom." Ellen eyed the mutilated bagel warily. "Sara Larsen wouldn't be worth your going to jail. Anyway, Ted also told me about how the students had gone through the steam tunnels and gotten into the nursing dorms."

"I remember that," Fannie laughed. "It was in all the papers, and they made a big to-do about closing down some of the tunnels and tightening security."

Ellen suddenly became very thoughtful. "You know, it's just a hunch, but in that Poe story where the Amontillado appears, there is a victim sealed behind a wall. It has given me an idea about the disappearance of Henry Dodson. It might be a place to begin. I wonder where I could go to find information about the buildings and Grounds of the University back then?"

"Only one place I can think of for that kind of information and that's Mr. Tippett. My cousin did yard work for him." Fannie smiled at the mention of the strange little man who was renowned for his encyclopedic knowledge of every bolt, faucet, and doorknob on the Grounds. Mr. Tippett had been in charge of Buildings and Grounds at the University from the 40's through the late 60's, when he finally retired with considerable comment on his part regarding the foolish new ways of doing things. Tippet didn't trust the "newfangled computerized" system being used for keeping the records.

When the University was still small, Mr. Tippett had kept information in his head and in battered file cabinets. Only he fully understood his "system" for keeping track of what was purchased or needed to be replaced. He was still consulted on occasions regarding things like plumbing connections or wiring that could not be traced and were not in the computer. The price one paid for information from him, however, was usually a diatribe against computerization and all the "newfangled ideas" about taking care of "his" institution. Over ninety, he still had a keen mind, and some of his concerns about low bids and state control had proven correct when buildings constructed in the 60's, with the very latest in roofing materials and climate control, began to leak copiously after a few years, and serious problems developed with the quality of the air.

"If you're ready for a lecture on what's wrong with the state of Virginia and UVa in particular, plus the world in general, then go have your chat with Mr. Tippett," Fannie said. "But maybe you'd better not start out by telling him that Poe story."

* * *

"Imagine constructing buildings with no windows that would open." Mr. Tippett leaned forward in his chair on the front porch of the retirement home where he had lived for several years.

"'Oh, the air conditioning will take care of the air, and we can't have people opening windows and messing up the system.' That is what they told me. Well, what do you think happened when the power went off? People just cooked in those buildings in the hot weather, that's what. And, what's more, the air is always stale. Now they have two or three of those buildings on the list as being 'sick.' Humph, it isn't the buildings that are sick. It's those dummies in Richmond that allowed such miserable structures to be built in the first place."

Mr. Tippett stopped long enough to get his breath, and Ellen quickly took advantage of the lull to ask her question. "Mr. Tippett, do you remember the incident with the nursing dorms, in the 60's, when the students sneaked in through the service tunnel and into the dorm? The University had some of the tunnels closed after that, I believe."

"Of course I remember," Mr. Tippett snapped. "I was in charge of the project. A lot of fuss about nothing, if you ask me, but the students were slipping around in those tunnels quite a bit in those days," he responded, with a rasping croak that may have been a chuckle. "Still are, I bet."

"Were there any tunnels that were actually sealed off so that they would permanently be put out of use?" Ellen inquired.

Mr. Tippett was quiet for a few moments, as he consulted his prodigious memory. "I think there were only two. Well, the one that lead to the nurses' dorm was sealed off, but only for a time. The other one was near the West Range and lead over to the Rotunda. The one to the Nursing dorm was eventually reopened, when new security measures with the entrances to the tunnels were put in. But I'm pretty sure that no one ever reopened the section leading to the Rotunda. It was closed at both ends and those steam pipes were rerouted."

"Mr. Tippett, do you have any recollection of exactly where that tunnel was sealed off?"

"Of course I remember. The opening to that tunnel is behind the last building on the West Range, just off the path. The main portion of the tunnel is still open, but the link to the Rotunda was sealed permanently."

"Mr. Tippett, you have been a big help. Thanks."

"Just remember this, Ellen. When you retire, a bureaucrat with a computer will replace you and things will never be the same again. You'll have to see your beloved University misused and abused." Mr. Tippett's voice broke, as he took Ellen's hand. She hugged the frail little man and knew that there was certainly a great deal of truth in what he said.

CHAPTER TWELVE

We continued our route in search of the Amontillado. We passed through a range of low arches, descended, passed on and descending again, arrived at a deep crypt . . .

—Poe's "The Cask of The Amontillado"

Ellen sat on one side of Mark's battered desk, thinking that surely the University could afford to buy a new one for its chief of police. Mark came back into the room from an emergency call he had been asked to take. His suit was rumpled and his shock of blonde hair was as unruly as usual. Even so, Ellen thought what a pleasant looking man he was. His eyes held a sadness and a loneliness that Ellen knew was connected to the loss of his wife. Ellen had known his former wife, Cindy, when she was a young woman. She came from a poor family and her father was a notorious drinker. Cindy had attached herself to Mark when they were kids, and he had taken care of her. Perhaps Cindy had felt that leaving was necessary to her survival, but she had nearly destroyed Mark.

"Sorry, Ellen. Somebody towed the Rector's car, and he was having a conniption. Now, what can I do for you?"

"Mark, please don't be angry with me, but I have been doing a little quiet investigating on my own, and I think there are some things you should know."

"Now, don't look at me like that," she said, in response to a deep frown that appeared on Mark's face. "Just hear me out before you start fussing at me."

Ellen told Mark about the events of the past few weeks and of her discussions with Ted Mitchell, Mr. Tippett, and Anne. However, she did not mention the parentage of Anne's child or the conversation with Reverend Evans. "I got one of the maintenance people to take me down into the service tunnel near the Rotunda, Mark, and that old wall that closes off the part of the passageway that used to lead to the Rotunda looks very unusual. The top third of the wall seems to have been completed by a different person than the lower part. It is a rougher job and not nearly so finished looking. The maintenance man said that perhaps the top of the wall was completed at a later time."

Mark started to interrupt, but Ellen hurried on. "I went back to see Mr. Tippett, and he said that he remembered the work on that wall had been delayed because of a fire in the Physics building, and when a crew returned to the tunnel, it had already been completed. They decided that some workman must have finished the wall during the interim and just hadn't filed a report. At any rate, they were still so busy cleaning up from the fire damage, they had no time to worry about who had finished the wall."

"Why is the completion of this wall of such interest to you, Ellen?" Mark said, in a puzzled voice.

"Because, Mark, that wall was built around the time of the disappearance of Henry Dodson. I'd like you to have that wall opened to see if there is any connection." She decided not to mention that the idea had come to her from Poe's short story.

"Ellen, you know that case is closed. What justification would I have in opening a case that is over thirty years old?"

"Use your imagination, Mark." Ellen leaned forward and touched Mark's arm. "You don't have to say why you are opening the wall. Just say that you have reason to suspect some stolen goods may have been hidden there. Say that someone spotted loose bricks down there and a small hole in the wall, and you suspect they may be using the tunnel as a hiding place. Take a small crew down to the tunnel and make an opening in the wall large enough to see on the other side."

Mark tapped his pencil on the desk. There shouldn't need to be an issue made of this. He could get a work crew down there without arousing any concern and that would be the end of it. Or would it? For a moment he had a premonition that the time might come when he would wish that he had not listened to Ellen.

But he shrugged off his misgivings. "All right, Ellen, I agree that what you have found out is at least worth a look. I will schedule a work order for next week."

CHAPTER THIRTEEN

The wall was now nearly upon a level with my breast. I again paused and holding the flambeaux over the mason-work threw a few feeble rays upon the figure within.
—Poe's "The Cask of the Amontillado"

If Bowman Ward had not been away at a meeting in Richmond the week that Mark took a crew down into the tunnels, things might have worked out very differently. The assistant who had taken Ward's place saw no reason to be concerned when Mark told him that he was going to open a small hole in one of the tunnel walls on Wednesday to investigate the possibility of stolen goods having been hidden there. "Sure, Mark, just have them patch up the damage," he had said. "I hope you find enough gold and jewels in there to pay for the shortfall in our budget next year."

Mark called Jake to ask if he would like to come down into the tunnel with him. When Jake arrived at his office, he looked at Mark quizzically. "I thought they warned you off of this case."

"What case?" Mark looked innocently at his friend. "We are just going down to investigate a strange looking part of a wall to see if anything might have been hidden there. You know the problems we have been having with petty thefts"

Jake looked at Mark quizzically. "Why do I think this ain't about cameras and portable radios?"

"To tell you the truth, Jake, Ellen spotted something suspicious about that wall, and I owe her this investigation. It's probably nothing, but she's a very smart lady, and I don't want to just ignore this possibility."

"This agreement we have between the city, the county, and

the University is important, Mark. We don't want to get in trouble for leaving the city out of the loop."

"I'll call Dexter as soon as I get back to the office, Jake. As far as we know now, this is just a routine check for missing goods and nothing of major concern to the city at this point."

"Well, our friend Dexter had a big smirk on his face when I saw him last week, and he was quick to tell me how he had heard the vice chancellor put an end to our so-called murder investigations, as he put it. I would sure like to know how he finds out so much about us."

"Dexter has made a career out of gathering information and using it to his own advantage. You wouldn't want to know what Dexter knows. He probably has a file on what you ate for breakfast."

"Yeah, well I hope warmed-over pizza from last night will give him some interesting data. It's sure given me indigestion," Jake laughed.

"Let's get out of here before he shows up. You're making me so paranoid, I have a feeling he already knows what we're planning to do." Mark picked up some papers and led the way out of the office.

Mark and Jake took three men with them, as they made their way through the narrow passage of the tunnel. When they came to the wall, they investigated the surface carefully with the beam from a large flashlight. It appeared to have been bricked over in two distinct parts, just as Ellen said. The bottom portion of the wall had a professional look and the top area was much rougher and uneven.

"Let's open a section in that top area large enough for me to get this flashlight in and have a look," Mark directed the men.

After several minutes of pounding and prying, enough bricks were dislodged that Mark could reach into the opening. He shone the light around inside, but saw nothing but the walls of the abandoned tunnel. "I can't quite see the floor area from this angle. Is there anything I could stand on?"

"I saw a step stool in the back of the truck," Jake said, and directed one of the men to go back to the truck and bring it down.

Climbing on the stool, Mark shone the light on the floor of the tunnel, but saw nothing unusual. He leaned in as far as possible and directed the beam against the inside surface of the wall at the bottom. It was then that the light glinted on an object on the floor. "It looks like something gold—maybe a ring, Jake."

Mark pulled his head out of the opening. "I need for the hole to be wider in order to get a good look in there. While we are working on this, one of you guys go back to the truck and see if we have a stronger light."

They all began to pry at the bricks around the hole. "Try to keep the debris from falling into the opening," Mark warned. The third officer returned, carrying a large flashlight, followed by the highly irritated Chief of the City Police, Dexter Paine, brushing dust from his impeccably tailored suit. Unlike Mark and Jake, Dexter never wore a uniform, except on special occasions.

"Whatever in the world is going on down here?" Dexter's high pitched voice never failed to grate on Mark.

"We are just investigating a suspicious-looking wall," Mark drawled.

"Suspicious-looking wall, indeed. When Bowman Ward's assistant mentioned that you were looking for stolen goods, I knew you were looking into that suicide again. Bowman has asked all of us to keep that business quiet and not cause any problems for the University, but you just won't be satisfied to let well enough alone." Dexter wiped the dust off his glasses and glared defiantly at his fellow officers of the law. "I shouldn't have to remind you of your responsibility."

"No, Dexter, you shouldn't. I invited Jake along to help me investigate this wall and that is exactly what we are going to do. If there is nothing unusual on the other side, then we can all go back to minding our own business."

Jake stifled a grin and spoke to one of the officers. "That hole looks big enough to me. What do you think, Mark?"

Mark turned his back on Dexter and climbed back on the stool, leaning as far inside the hole as possible in order to shine his light where he had seen the gold. Suddenly he froze, as the light glinted once again on what was definitely a gold ring.

"My God," he said. "You aren't going to believe this."

The ring was encircling one of the fingers of a skeletal hand, and Mark could just make out the University of Virginia emblem engraved on the front of the ring.

Mark drew out his head and turned toward the waiting men. "We will have to do some careful research. But, if I'm not mistaken, I think we may have just located the missing Henry Dodson."

* * *

Ellen was waiting in her office, trying to keep her mind on her work and not on the activity in the tunnel. At ten o'clock, Mark called.

"We found a body, Ellen, just as you thought. And Ellen, there was a UVa ring on one of the finger bones that had Henry Dodson's name engraved on it. Apparently, he had been murdered, and then his body was taken to the tunnel and placed behind the wall. It looks like the murderer noticed the wall under construction and planned to take the body there. He may even have set the fire in the physics building to delay the completion of the wall. After the body was lifted inside the opening, the murderer finished putting the bricks in place with mortar."

Ellen sighed, with a mixture of relief that her hunch had proven to be correct and sadness at the reality of murder on the Grounds. "What will you do next, Mark?"

"I have already called the vice chancellor, and he was none too pleased with the news. He has no choice, however, but to order a full-scale investigation of both deaths. There is no way to sweep a skeleton under the carpet—too lumpy." Mark grinned at his own rare attempt at humor.

Ellen started to request of Mark that he be sensitive in dealing with Anne and Sarah, but then she realized that Bowman Ward would take care of that situation, since he had already gone to some lengths in the past to protect Reverend Evans and his family.

"Mark, please keep me informed about what is going on. Also let me know if I can be of help to you."

"I will be over tomorrow to find out what you already know, Ellen. If it had not been for you, both of these deaths would have been forgotten."

CHAPTER FOURTEEN

Once upon a midnight dreary, while I pondered weak and weary, over many a quaint and curious volume . . .

—Poe's "The Raven"

The long, sticky summer dragged on through the month of September and the return of the students for the fall semester. Ellen went away for two weeks to Sand Bridge to visit her cousin, as she did every summer, but the sea breezes were quickly forgotten on her return to Charlottesville. Hot and humid days gave way to hot and even more humid nights, in which the air conditioner labored to bring some comfort. At last, the cool nights and warm days of October arrived, and people in Charlottesville remembered once again why they enjoyed living in the Piedmont of Virginia. The leaves of the trees on the Blue Ridge Mountains in the distance, and the Ragged Mountains nearby, turned the warm, sun-drenched colors of autumn, and at night the moon hung luminous over the town.

Ellen and Fannie were savoring the cool breeze on her patio during their Saturday morning brunch. The dogwood trees at the edge of her tiny yard were a brilliant red, and the maple leaves on the street were just beginning to be touched with a bright yellow-orange.

"I just love this time of the year. I think the colors will stay beautiful for a few weeks, after all that rain we had in September." Ellen stretched lazily in her chaise lounge.

"It will have to be beautiful to make up for this summer. I nearly cooked in my trailer and fans didn't do anything but move the heat around." Fannie passed a plate of warm sticky buns to

Ellen and brushed away a lazy fly that was trying to fall over into her coffee cup.

"If I inherited a pot full of gold, the first thing I would do is buy you an air conditioner," Ellen said.

"Hey, the first thing you *should* do is go and put a down payment on that tea room you keep dreaming about and put me to work—then I can pay for my own air conditioner!" Fannie put an exclamation point to her statement by smacking the fly with the newspaper.

"I've been looking at my savings and, without some angel appearing with a bag full of money, there is not enough to get us started."

"I wish I had something to contribute besides my recipes—and this pretty face—but there's no money in my piggy bank." Fannie got up and poured them some more coffee. "Well, enough daydreaming. What's the latest you've heard about the case?"

"I just wish that Mark would call me with some news. They've hit a dead-end, I'm afraid," Ellen sighed, thinking of the possibility that they would never know what happened.

"What'd he tell you when he was over last week?"

"Not much. They've interviewed all those who are known to be connected with this case several times. He and Jake had them into the office, or they went out to visit with each of them. Some were very cooperative, but others were less so—like Reverend Evans. Mark said that he was really appreciative of Jake's help and support. The vice chancellor kept insisting that Dexter be included in the process, and Mark was able to say that too many people involved in an interrogation was unfair to the witnesses. I think Mark didn't want Dexter around any more than absolutely necessary. He and Jake never say very much about Dexter, but I get the distinct impression that they would rather not work with him, if they had the choice."

"Friends of mine who have been in the police department for years say that he is a disaster as a police chief, but the politicians just keep covering up for him because of his old man's money. One of these days he is going to get found out. I just hope that people don't get hurt because of him."

"The trouble is that almost everyone who knew Henry Dodson had a reason to want him dead. It's difficult to establish a motive unless they all formed a pact and had him removed, like the passengers did on the Orient Express." Ellen took a second bun, refusing to consider the number of calories oozing out of the pastry.

"How does Mark think the murderer got Charlie to go into that room and drink that wine?" Fannie asked, frowning. "From what you say about him, no one could have forced him to go in there."

"Mark thinks that one of the people whom Charlie approached about the secret society invited him to go through the ritual. Perhaps the person told Charlie that he would be inducted in the society and that the others were going to be waiting for him after the ceremony. Charlie would have loved being part of such a ritual and of such a society. It would have appealed to the romantic side of his nature that was drawn to Poe's writing. Charlie would have thought it a lark—a fun thing to do. Why he even told me he wanted to start the society up again. According to the instructions for the initiation, the wine in the room was to be Amontillado, like in one of Poe's stories. You know, in that story the murderer buried his victim alive inside a brick wall. It's ironic that it was that story that gave us the clue as to the whereabouts of Henry Dodson."

"Well, that seems to mean that it had to be one of the members of that society," Fannie pointed out. "Sure narrows the list of suspects."

"I said the same thing to Mark, but he pointed out that other people may have known about the society, and one of the members may have sent Charlie to see them—although they all deny having done so—or Charlie may have spoken to others, just as he spoke to me. We don't know whom he talked to about his discovery of the box. He could have decided to act all of this out with another person whom we still don't know. I believe that there must be a connection between Henry Dodson, the blackmailer, and what Charlie was about to discover, or what the murderer was afraid Charlie might uncover."

"Did you have anything to offer Mark when you saw him? I thought you were going to tell him about the numbers on that scrap of paper that had been buried with the other papers."

"Mark didn't seem to think that it was anything important. He thought it was probably just something Henry Dodson had jotted down that had no connection to the murder."

"Well, why did he have it hidden in that little box then, if it wasn't important?" Fannie did not entirely trust any of the police working on the case—even Mark.

"I asked him the same thing, but Mark just didn't seem to think he could possibly put any meaning to it."

"Go and get the message and a pad of paper and let's look at it again," Fannie said. Ellen went to her desk and drew out the piece of paper on which she had written the strange message.

Fannie produced a stub of a pencil from her sweater pocket and handed it to Ellen. "Write it on here in big letters," Fannie directed.

Ellen copied the following onto the napkin.

P S—26—02—I 6—84

Fannie looked at the series for several minutes, turning the envelope in different directions. "I wonder if this is a code—some way of remembering words or letters in some order. When I was a kid, we were always inventing secret codes. Remember when you could send off for a secret ring with coded messages to hide inside? It was some radio show we all listened to."

"I think it was Jack Armstrong or Ranger Rick." Ellen mused.

"Does that look like anything to you?" Fannie said, turning the napkin around so that she could see it clearly.

"It reminds me of something, but I don't know what. Maybe it really is just some nonsense and of no importance, like Mark said."

An hour later, they still had not resolved the mystery. "My eyes are nearly crossed with staring at this, and so far we haven't made any sense out of it. Let's go for a walk and forget codes in favor of cones. How about rum raisin?"

* * *

A few nights later, Ellen couldn't sleep. She awoke at two in the morning and found herself staring wide-eyed into the darkness. A cup of warm milk and relaxation exercises didn't help. Finally, she turned on the light and decided to read until she was sleepy. A stack of library books was piled on her desk, and she lifted one at a time to see what might be inviting, but not too exciting. She decided against a Father Cadfael mystery—too stimulating—she would be awake all night with that book for sure—and a book about Matisse—too strenuous for two in the morning. A collection of short stories by Peter Taylor, one of her favorite writers and a University professor until his death, seemed just the thing. She carried the book back to bed, turned up the bedside light for reading, and then settled herself comfortably on the pillows. She turned the book over to see the cover, and her eyes were drawn to the white library tab on the side of the spine.

PS 3539 A 9633

She should have been too excited to sleep, but the discovery of the probable answer to the mystery of the slip of paper in the box worked like a charm, and she was sound asleep in minutes.

CHAPTER FIFTEEN

Thomas Jefferson began planning for the University's library in 1819 by selecting books for the collections and writing rules for their use . . .

University of Virginia Library Facts at a Glance

The next day, Ellen left her desk at lunch time and walked to the library. It was raining, and puddles had formed between the bricks in the walk. The gray day made her confidence shrink, and she wondered if it would be better to let Mark handle the investigation and mind her own business. Still, she had never given up on a job to be done. Why shouldn't she check out her theory before involving Mark and wasting his time? After all, it was Mark who thought the numbers were unimportant. A little part of her wanted to show him just how clever she could be. She pushed open the door to the library with renewed determination.

Her friend, Susan Ames, in reference examined the numbers carefully. Ellen had written the numbers to look more like a library reference—PS 2602 I 684.

"These appear to be call numbers, just as you thought," Susan said. "I believe this could be a Poe book in the rare book collection. Let me just check here on the computer to be sure." A few clicks later, the screen verified the location of the book in the rare book section.

"Wait just a minute and I will walk downstairs with you. I need a break."

It had been years since Ellen had walked down the two flights of stairs in the library to the area where the rare books were housed. They entered the elegantly furnished and softly lit reading room that was a marked contrast to the bare utilitarian passage that led to it. Susan asked one of the attendants to bring them the book, and they sat in the comfortable leather chairs.

"What does the 'I' mean in that call letter?" Ellen asked. "I thought this was a collection of Poe's writings."

"The 'I' means that the preface to the collection was written by a man whose last name began with an 'I,'" replied Susan. "In this case, it was John Ingram. He is of major interest now, since his letters to Poe's fiancée and hers to him have just been published."

The young man returned bearing a book titled *The Poems and Essays of Edgar Allan Poe, Introduction by John H. Ingram*, which he handed to Ellen. "I have no idea what I am looking for. If it is all right with you, I will just sit here for a while and look through the book to see if I notice anything."

"I'll go back upstairs," Susan said. "Just call if you need me and be sure to stop by the desk before you leave. I may need a coffee break by that time."

Ellen settled herself in the comfortable leather chair and opened the book. The date of publication was 1876, and she relished the wonderful old book smell that floated up from the yellowed pages. What could I possibly find by just looking at this book? she thought to herself, feeling faintly foolish.

* * *

Thirty minutes later, Ellen was surrounded by agitated library officials and Susan, who was carefully examining the book and taking notes. Ellen pointed out to them where several pages had been cut very skillfully from the preface. "Only a person who was carefully examining the text would notice the missing pages," Ellen said. "They could have been gone for many years."

"Should we call in the police?" Susan inquired of the library director, who had been hastily summoned when the missing pages were reported.

"Let me just look into this matter quietly first. We had so much notoriety about those illustrations that were cut from rare books and then sold that I would like to keep this quiet. After all, this is not a particularly valuable book and the missing pages could not contain anything that would be of interest to a collector." He hurried away, clutching the damaged book as though it might explode.

Ellen and Susan climbed back up the stairs. "I will have to tell Mark Pace about this, Susan, because it may be relevant to a case he's working on. I'm sure he will be discreet."

"Oh, that's all right, Ellen. You know how paranoid the University is about publicity. The more they try to avoid it and keep everything quiet, the more they seem to get." Susan sighed, as she went back into her office and sat behind the desk, motioning to Ellen to take a seat.

"I just wish I could get hold of another copy of that book. Do you know if there are any more in existence?" Ellen asked.

Susan reached behind her in the cabinet and extracted a manila folder. "A number of Poe books were donated to the library at Boston University, and they sent us the information regarding those rare books that we had copies of in our collection. Perhaps the Ingram book was among those they listed."

"Is there any way I could see that book?" Ellen inquired.

"They'd have placed it in their rare book collection, but I know the librarian there. If they have it, I think that she would send it to us on loan for a short period of time. Let me call her and I'll let you know."

"Thank you, Susan, you have been a tremendous help, as always." Ellen gave her friend a brief hug. "May I use your phone to call Mark and see if he can meet me at the coffee shop so that I can let him know about this?"

When Mark said he could be there in about twenty minutes, Ellen left the library to walk towards the coffee shop. She did not notice the city police chief enter as she was leaving, nor did she notice that he watched her with a strange look on his face. He turned inside the door and made his way to Susan's desk. "Susan, was that Ellen Randolph I saw leaving just now?" Dexter was not very generous with polite greetings unless he was ingratiating himself to someone he considered of importance.

"Yes, it was, Dexter. Why do you ask?"

"Someone called us from downstairs about the damage to the library book she was reading. Why haven't you called to make an official report?"

"Really, Dexter, we don't call the police to report every book that has some missing pages. Anyway, this is a matter for the University police. I'm sure Mark would have contacted you."

"My source said this was not just *any* book, but a book from the rare book room." Dexter took out his notebook and settled himself into the nearest chair. "Now, would you please give me a full account, Susan. I'll call Mark personally."

CHAPTER SIXTEEN

Those stories of his misconduct were the invention of an inimical and jealous biographer, the Reverend Rufus Griswold . . . examples of the biographist's mendacity.

"Edgar Allan Poe at the University—1826"

By Irby B. Cauthen, Jr.

Ellen had a few minutes before she was to meet Mark, so she decided to do something that she had been avoiding for too long.

She turned to her right, after crossing the road from the library, and walked to the Poe room. All signs of death and suffering were gone. Everything had been restored to its accustomed order. The bed was made again, with the coverlet in place. The writing desk holding the pen and ink and the open book was there, but this copy probably had no words underlined containing a possible final communication from a desperate young man about to take his own life.

Ellen pushed the button for the recorded message and, to her surprise, it was working. The mellifluous tones of one of the University's leading thespians rolled out of the speaker.

> **The young Poe was an avid reader and an excellent student of the modern languages. His translations in French were remembered as being outstanding and precisely correct. He also studied Italian and Spanish and was singled out by his professor as being the only student to complete a difficult translation. At the end of the ten months Poe spent at the University, he had excelled in the examinations of both Latin and French. He was also an outstanding athlete adept at all gymnastic exercises; a skilled debater serving as the**

> secretary of the debating society; and a superb storyteller, who kept students spellbound in his room reading from his strange and wild creations.
>
> There is no record in the University that he was ever in any trouble with the school due to his behavior. In fact, the librarian of the university at that time spoke of Poe as "a sober and quiet young man." Several times, he was invited to have dinner with Mr. Jefferson together with other outstanding students. Poe's guardian did not give him adequate funds on which to live, and then forced him to leave the University when his debts mounted.
>
> Poe died, just as he was about to achieve a degree of security that he had not known in his life, having been orphaned at the age of three and having known little stability in his forty years. The popular version of his death had him drinking himself into a drunken stupor after a night of revelry and collapsing in the snow—a victim of his own weakness and drunkenness. Another, and quite different, story describes Poe as the innocent victim of thugs who had been hired to drug voters and take them around to various polling places. It was an election night and Poe might have been left unconscious in the snow by his abductors. When found, he was taken to a hospital, where he died from exposure without gaining consciousness and without ever being able to explain what had happened.
>
> Many biographers had assumed the worse, that he collapsed in a drunken stupor, but there might have been another explanation, had Poe been able to defend himself.

Ellen thought of Charlie and how he had come into her office with such enthusiasm and vigor. Would he be remembered as a despondent student who took his life in a strange and bizarre way—if he were remembered at all—or would he be described as a promising young scholar who had his life taken from him prematurely and violently?

I don't know the answer yet, Charlie, Ellen murmured to herself, as she turned sadly away from the room, but I intend to find out.

* * *

"If this is what I think it is, Mark, it could be the clue we need as to why someone wanted Henry Dodson dead." Ellen was out of breath, after having hurried to meet Mark upon leaving the Poe room. Mark had a worried frown on his face, which Ellen tried to ignore.

"All of the men in the secret society were doing research related in some way to the life and work of Poe. There must be something in that library book that will lead us to the person or persons willing to commit two murders to keep anyone from finding out what they were doing." Ellen stopped in her breathless report. "What's the matter, Mark? Don't you think this is the breakthrough we've been looking for?"

Mark pulled his chair closer to Ellen's and lowered his voice. "I think it may very well be exactly what you say, and that is what has me worried. I wish you hadn't gone to the library by yourself. In this town, word can get out so easily about what you are doing."

"Oh, for heaven's sake. I didn't want to bother you unless there really *was* something to the call numbers. I only talked to my friend in the reserved book collection. She isn't going to tell anyone," replied Ellen, but she had lowered her voice and leaned closer to Mark.

"Ellen, in a case like this, where people are involved who have prominence and power, you don't know who may mention something without realizing what they may be doing. Jake called just a few minutes after you did to tell me that Dexter Paine was on his way to the library to inquire about the damaged book you discovered. He was irate that we were planning to keep things 'undercover,' as he put it."

"Good heavens, Mark. I will be more careful, but I think you are worrying for nothing. After all, Dexter's just doing his job, even if he does do it in an unpleasant manner at times. But, who in the world called Dexter?"

"I'm not sure, but you have to promise me not to make any other moves without calling me first. This is very serious business, Ellen."

* * *

Two days later, Ellen was working at her desk when a doctoral student who had once been a guide stopped in her office.

"I'm on my way to turn in the first draft of my dissertation, and I just wanted to celebrate with someone who cares. What a relief to have gotten this far." The student placed the dissertation on Ellen's desk and stepped back to view it proudly. "I can hardly wait until I'm finally done and it is bound and on the shelf in the library with my name on the cover."

Ellen also gazed at the manuscript, but with a different expression on her face. "Do they have all of the dissertations on the library shelves?"

"As far as I know, they do. At least those for the College of Arts and Science."

"What about masters' theses in English? Are they in the library as well?" Ellen's voiced betrayed her excitement.

"Yes, I think so. Wait—yes—I am sure they are there. I used a couple of them in my research. They are in the same section as the dissertations. Why do you ask, Mrs. Randolph?"

"There's something I have been intending to look up, and I had not realized that the master's theses were in the library. This is a help to me."

"I'm glad my dissertation has been a help to someone. Anyway, I had better get this over to my advisor before he decides I need to stay for another year and work for slave wages as a graduate assistant. Goodbye, and thanks for everything. You've been a real friend."

Ellen sat at her desk for several minutes. Finally, she called to the secretary to tell her that she was going out for a while to eat her lunch in the garden and then go to the library, and she would not be back for about two hours.

Ellen was about to ignore Mark's admonition, with nearly disastrous consequences.

CHAPTER SEVENTEEN

Deep into that darkness peering, long I stood there wondering, fearing . . .

—*Poe's "The Raven"*

It was a beautiful day, as Ellen walked from the garden to the library. She had taken her time eating her lunch in the warm sun, savoring the opportunity to check out her theory about the masters' theses. The leaves of the ginko trees, which were brought to America by Mr. Jefferson, had turned a bright yellow, and the stinky fruit from the female trees, that look like apricots, had almost disappeared from the sidewalks. Ellen wondered why Mr. Jefferson would bring a tree to his new university that bore a fruit that smelled like vomit when tracked into warm classrooms on the shoes of students. Sometimes, she suspected the noble gentleman of having a warped sense of humor.

The oaks and maples were a blaze of color against the blue autumn sky, and the dark green of the tall pines seemed especially intense beside their brilliance. The uncertainty she had felt on her last trip to the library was gone. She felt full of energy, striding along the walk, speaking to some of the students. Mark's warning to her regarding the possible dangers in her involvement seemed almost silly, as she looked about the familiar and beloved scene.

Ellen went into the library and approached the reference desk where Hiram Perkins, the reference librarian, was busily sorting cards. "Good afternoon, Hiram. Could you tell me where the doctoral dissertations and masters' theses in English Literature are shelved?"

The little man looked at her over his spectacles, with the vaguely suspicious look he reserved for all objects in the universe that were not books. "They are on the first floor to the left of the elevator, Ellen. You will find them arranged by subject and year. The elevator down that hall and to the left will take you to that area."

As Ellen waited for the elevator, she heard a rumble of thunder in the distance and noticed that the sunlight had disappeared from the windows. It had become darker inside the building and Ellen had a strange feeling of foreboding, which she dismissed as just her usual unease when a storm was brewing. When she emerged from the elevator, the first floor seemed very quiet. No students were studying at the tables, and the lights were turned off in the stacks. Ellen had never been to this floor of the library. It looked like a place for storing things meant to be forgotten.

She wandered around for a few minutes and finally located the English section of the dissertations and then, just beyond them, the masters' theses. Ellen turned on the lights in her part of the stacks from a switch on the end of the corridor. Rain was beginning to spatter the windows and the room was nearly dark.

She had written the names of all the men in the society on a piece of paper, in order to locate their theses. These were filed in alphabetical order by year, and she went down the shelf until she located the space where Anthony Antonetti's thesis should be located, but there was no copy with his name on it in the appropriate spot. She looked for the theses of George Blake, John Grieco, Frank Gruver, and Arnold Theodore Mitchell. They were also missing. Apparently, she surmised someone may have gone through the shelves and systematically removed all the copies.

Ellen thought that when she went upstairs, she would look on the computer to see if the theses had been checked out. If not, the copies would have to have been hidden or destroyed inside the library, since there were detectors at each of the exits. She decided to look one more time within a range of four or five years, to make certain that she had not overlooked any of the copies, when suddenly the lights were switched off, leaving the entire area in near darkness.

At first, Ellen assumed that someone had come through and turned off the light in her area, thinking it had been left on by mistake, but she did not hear anyone moving along the main corridor, nor had she heard the elevator. Of course, there were stairs to all of the floors, but the library personnel would most likely use the elevator. The only other way for the lights to be turned off would be from the main switch for the entire floor, but she had not heard anyone while she had been in the stacks.

Suddenly, Ellen felt fear prickle along the back of her neck like an electric charge and she stood very still, leaning against the shelves, and listened. There had been a sound at the far end of the stacks against the back wall. She was not alone. Gradually, her eyes were adjusting to the dim light. Then she heard a very faint movement, as though someone were coming down the aisle in her direction, but walking very carefully. The rain on the windows and the rumble of thunder momentarily blocked the sound, but then she heard it again, and this time it was closer.

Ellen peered through the space between the books and the top of the shelf. A figure moved slowly along the side aisle from the rear, stopped at the end of the aisle, and then moved on. Someone was looking for her, and Ellen felt terror begin to take over her mind. She touched the locket around her neck, but realized that it was only gold and glass. The pictures inside it, of her husband and daughter, could not help in this situation.

She moved carefully around the end of the stack and tried to collect her thoughts. There was only one main aisle leading to the elevator. If she came out of the stacks on that aisle, she would be visible to the person stalking her. She could work her way around the end of the stacks, but eventually she would have to come out in the open to reach the elevator.

Quickly, she moved around each of the stacks towards the elevator, but the other person seemed to anticipate her intention. She could hear the steps, less cautious now, moving along the aisle in her direction. Then another sound attracted her attention—the low hum of the elevator. If she could get there in time and press the button, perhaps she could get the elevator to stop at this floor. But what if her pursuer also heard the hum and got on the elevator with her before the door closed? It was a chance she would have to take. The stairs were on the other side of the elevator, and there was no access to them from where she was without going down the main aisle. She moved as fast as possible toward the sound of the elevator and burst out of the aisle with her fingers frantically seeking the button.

From down the aisle, she heard the footsteps moving in her direction. Even if the door opened, she was still easy prey for someone who was quick enough to jump into an empty elevator behind her. As the doors opened, she felt the presence of someone very near and nearly fell through the opening, hoping to get the door closed in time.

"Good heavens, Ellen. Whatever is the matter?" Ellen suppressed the desire to throw her arms around the nervous, bespectacled Mr. Perkins.

"It is all right now, Hiram. I just had a little—uh—spell of dizziness. I'll be fine."

"If you wish, I could accompany you back to the main floor. Just let me put these books down for the bindery."

"No, please, Hiram, don't bother." Ellen pressed the button to the main floor, with a prayer of thanks on her lips.

She stopped in the ladies' lounge to sit for a moment and collect her thoughts. Her knees were still shaking from fear. She rested her head on the back of the leather sofa and closed her eyes, trying to make some sense of what had just occurred, but she sat up abruptly as the door opened and her friend Susan entered the room.

"Ellen, Mr. Perkins said you weren't feeling well, and he saw you come in here. Are you all right?"

"Well, I think I am, Susan. It may have been my imagination, but it seemed to me that someone was stalking me when I was in the stacks downstairs."

"Good heavens, do you want me to call the police?"

"No, as I said, it could have been my imagination. I'll talk to Mark about it." Ellen was remembering what Mark had said about talking too much in public places.

"What were you doing down there, anyway?" Susan asked

"I was checking for some masters' theses, which I didn't find." Ellen began to gather her things. If she stayed much longer, she would probably blurt out the whole story.

"Does this have anything to do with that damaged book you found, Ellen?" Susan was not going to be easily put off.

"It may be, indirectly. It's just a hunch I had that probably doesn't mean much."

"Well, I don't like the idea that someone may have been after you. I think you should report this immediately."

"I promise to talk about it to Mark, Susan. Thanks for worrying about me, but I am sure it was nothing serious."

As soon as Ellen was out of the building, Susan picked up the phone and called Dexter Paine. When he had left her office the previous week, he had made it very clear that she was to report anything unusual to him, and only to him. Susan didn't want him reappearing in her office and speaking to her as though she had been an accessory to some crime.

Dexter Paine listened to Susan's report of the incident without comment. As usual, he didn't bother to express any appreciation for her call and hung up the telephone abruptly when she had finished. Then he picked it up again and dialed a familiar number.

CHAPTER EIGHTEEN

And much of Madness, and more of Sin,
And Horror the soul of the plot.
—Poe's "The Conqueror Worm"

"I warned you about this, Ellen, but you have refused to listen. How could you have taken such an unnecessary risk?"

Mark strode up and down the narrow space in her office, rubbing his forehead in exasperation, while Ellen looked meekly on.

"I admit I've been very foolish, Mark. It just didn't occur to me that I could be in real danger. After all, I know these people. This is my home—these are my friends."

"Not everyone out there is your friend, Ellen, and you may be in danger. I wish you would reconsider my suggestion that you go away for a while."

"I just can't do that, Mark. For one thing, this is the busiest time of the year for fundraising, and we need to work extremely hard this year to pay for some needed restorations. Besides, I refuse to run away. I'm just too old and set in my ways to become a helpless victim." She paused for a moment, "But I promise you that I won't be so foolish again."

"Dexter Paine was in the vice chancellor's office, insisting that you be put on some type of administrative leave—'for your own good.' I told them that such an action would not only be unacceptable to you, but unlawful as well. Fortunately, the vice chancellor had to agree with me, although reluctantly." Mark rubbed his eyes in fatigue.

"I know," Ellen sighed. "Bowman tried to convince me to take a leave, with a number of veiled threats, but I told him there is no way I am going to be frightened away by him, or by anyone else." As Ellen stuck out her chin, Mark thought she looked like a determined little girl. He had to work hard to keep from smiling.

"I don't like the way that arrogant Dexter and that pompous Bowman Ward act like they're in charge of the universe. Why are they working together on this, when this is your territory?"

"Well, Dexter is the city chief of police and he is on much friendlier terms with the vice chancellor than Jake or me. I guess they communicate with each other better." Mark was thinking that Dexter had always been more willing to do what the vice chancellor wanted than either of the other two police officers. He had even been willing, on occasions, to withhold information or protect the son or daughter of some influential alumnus at Bowman's request.

"I have instructed your staff not to give out any information regarding your whereabouts. According to the detectives who questioned them, the person who stalked you in the library may have called several times asking for you and then hung up before the call was transferred to your phone. The staff had no reason to be suspicious and thought that it was simply a person who had decided not to wait. The voice was somewhat muffled, so they could not tell whether it was a man or a woman, but the last time the person called, he—or she—was told you were in the library. That was very helpful information, obviously." Ellen heard the fear behind the sarcasm in Mark's voice.

"I never thought to say anything to the staff about guarding my whereabouts. They couldn't have anticipated a problem," Ellen said. "For that matter, neither did I."

"I have asked Dexter to have your home under surveillance by the city police, and a university police person will be on duty outside the door to your office. Now, don't worry." For the first time, Mark allowed a smile to crack his serious expression. "The person will be in plain clothes, so as not to frighten your precious donors."

"Mark, please don't react negatively to what I am about to say before you get a chance to think it over." Ellen reached out and touched him on the arm. "Since I may already be in danger, and most likely known by the murderer to be involved, let me help you in any way that I can." Ellen hurried on before Mark could interrupt. "There are a few things I might do for you that no one else could do as well. It is possible that the murderer has destroyed all the library copies of the masters' theses belonging to the members of the secret society. The same person probably removed the pages from the book in the rare book collection, so those theses must have some connection to the murders. He or she—although it would have to be a very strong she—probably feels relatively safe now. However, I know where there is a copy of one of the theses, and I think I could get it for you."

Mark stopped his pacing and looked at her in surprise. "What are you talking about, Ellen? I thought you said that all of the copies had been removed from the library shelves."

"I saw a copy of Ted's master's thesis on the shelf in his study next to his doctoral dissertation, when I visited him. I could go back to see Ted and ask him to loan me the copy. If Ted were to be the guilty person, then he already knows about me. If he is not, then it will seem like a relatively innocuous request. This way, you will have one thesis to compare to the material in the library book when it arrives from Boston and, when you have cleared Ted, you can ask his help in locating the other copies and determining what may be of interest in the text."

Mark looked doubtful, as he considered the possibilities of Ellen's proposal, and said, "I'll agree—only if you let me know exactly when you plan to go to Ted's, so I can be close by."

"It's a promise." Ellen was relieved that Mark was no longer angry with her. She had gradually come to enjoy having him around and even to appreciate being taken care of by this very agreeable and attractive young man.

CHAPTER NINETEEN

Always write first things uppermost in the heart.

—Poe's "Elizabeth"

Fannie and Ellen were inside the house, in front of a welcome fire, enjoying muffins from a local bakery, since Fannie had been "down in the back," as she put it, and unable to bake. A cold November wind was blowing the remaining leaves around the patio and rain was in the forecast.

"No wonder my back has been bothering me, with all this rain we've been having. I don't like November, even if it is your birthday month."

Ellen reached for another blueberry muffin and spread it with butter. "When I was a little girl, I believed that my birthday came early in November to brighten the month and help people make it to Thanksgiving—like St. Valentine's Day in February."

"Well, you can go around comparing yourself to a saint, if you want to, but that isn't going to keep you out of trouble if you insist on poking that nose of yours into this murder case." Fannie glowered at her friend over the rim of the coffee cup, genuine concern evident in her voice.

"Mark is being very careful about how I poke my nose around, as you put it. I tell you, Fannie, if I were thirty years younger—Hmmmm."

Fannie was not to be put off by Ellen's attempts to lighten the subject. "Never mind if you were thirty years younger. I'm more concerned with you getting any older. Somebody out there may be trying to get rid of you, and it makes goose bumps break out all over me just thinking about it. That person could be out there, right now, watching for an opportunity to get to you."

"There is a policeman on duty. I think he's over there in that parked car, and I have a beeper right here to let him know if I'm in any trouble." Ellen reached into her sweater pocket and then drew out her hand, without a beeper, a puzzled look on her face. "It was in here last evening. I must have left it on the bedside table."

"Oh, fine. The beeper will do you a lot of good on the bedside table if you're downstairs in the living room. You see, you aren't taking this seriously enough."

"I really am, Fannie. I just can't let fear run my life. I promise to keep my beeper with me constantly from now on and not take any unnecessary chances. That event in the library really did make me aware of how serious all this is, but it also made me realize that I can think through a situation and take care of myself, even when I'm very frightened. I don't feel as vulnerable, in some ways, as I did before. I'm still furious about having someone tracking me like an animal in those stacks."

"Well, what do you plan to do next with all this newfound bravery?" Fannie's voice was still full of concern for her friend.

Ellen told her about the plan to get the thesis from Ted. "We are still waiting for the copy of the book to arrive from Boston. I just don't know how we will be able to determine what in the book is important in finding the murderer. None of us are Poe scholars. I'm hoping that if we can clear Ted from any suspicion, he will help us search for the clue we need in the text."

"It's really hard for me to believe that he had anything to do with this murder," Fannie replied. "He's not one of my favorite people. Etta Mae says he sure is full of himself, but I don't think he could poison anybody. But, you just never know how far somebody like that might go to protect himself," Fannie added thoughtfully.

"Speaking of Etta, that sister of yours put on the biggest 'Step n' Fetchit' shuffle, when she was serving tea at Ted's, that I've ever witnessed. It was practically a 'yassuh boss, what can this ole darkie do fo you' performance. What is going on there?"

"Oh, she just loves to do that with him, and he eats it up. She heard him tell someone one day that she was one of the few black folk he knew with really good manners. If he only knew. She can do an imitation of him pretending to be the dutiful husband that would knock your socks off."

"I wonder if Ted has always had a roving eye or did it just come after he married Rebecca?" Ellen said, pouring herself some more coffee from the carafe.

"I'm going to tell you something, Ellen, that is really a trade secret. Some of that act Etta Mae puts on is a defense against him looking at her as a woman. As long as she shuffles around and says 'yassuh boss,' he sees her as a servant with no real personality of her own. She wouldn't admit it, of course, but I know several women who do housework who use that defense when they are alone with a man like Ted. Of course, if he'd ever try anything he'd get the surprise of his life. Etta Mae is plenty tough, but heck, she also needs the work. Right now, with her children in school, she can't afford to lose that job."

"I've often wondered about that," Ellen replied sadly. "I remember once when my father-in-law was visiting us, many years ago, I came in the room unexpectedly and found him with his arm around the shoulders of a young woman I had hired as a sitter. She had a very uncomfortable look on her face and, of course, he brushed it off with a laugh and some comment about protecting sweet young things, but it sure made me feel uneasy. In fact, I tried not to leave him in the house alone with any woman or girl ever again." Ellen sighed and got up to look out of the window at her official guardian. "Some people never change."

But Ellen was wrong. Her attitude toward Ted Mitchell's character was about to change dramatically.

CHAPTER TWENTY

Well I may venture so far as to say that the paper gives its holder a certain power . . .

—Poe's "The Purloined Letter"

On the day she had scheduled the visit with Ted, Ellen left the office and met Mark at the front of the Rotunda. It was a cold, late November morning. An early light snow was blowing across the Lawn, etching the tree trunks with a fine white powder.

"Where are you going to wait for me?" Ellen asked Mark, taking his arm, as they walked down the colonnade, just beginning to be slick with the blowing snow.

"I'm going to wait in the Colonnade Club, just inside the door. I can keep an eye on Professor Mitchell's Pavilion from there. If you aren't out in half an hour, I am going to ring the bell on some pretext."

"This shouldn't take very long. I'll be out before you get warmed up from this cold wind."

Ellen walked briskly to the door to Ted's pavilion and rang the bell. It was some time, however, before he opened the door. "Good morning, dear Ellen. How nice to see you."

Was she imagining things, or was Ted's greeting somewhat forced? Ellen thought she must be getting paranoid about everything at this point. "Good morning, Ted. It's nice of you to see me."

"It's Etta Mae's day off, so I regret that I cannot offer you something warm to take away the chill." He bustled about, hanging up her coat.

Ellen wondered if Ted ever ventured into his own kitchen to make a cup of tea. "Thank you, Ted. I just wanted to ask a favor of you."

Once again, Ted led her into his study, and this time he sat behind his massive mahogany desk. Ellen felt suddenly like a schoolgirl being summoned to the principal's office, but she was too old to fall for such an obvious power play. She walked around the desk and took a chair near the window on his side of the desk, causing him to turn and face her without the desk between them. "Two of us can play at this game," she thought, "but why is there a game being played at all?"

"I wonder if I might I borrow a copy of your master's thesis for a few days, Ted. All this talk about the past has made me interested in the work you did on Poe, particularly since you were one of Robert's most outstanding students. Since all this came up about a secret society, I've been interested in reading more about the work you and the others were doing at that time. I can't help being curious. Sometimes I just yearn to recapture part of the past." Ellen had gone over in her mind very carefully how she could ask Ted for the dissertation without telling a lie. "The library copy of your thesis seems to be missing."

"Oh, my, how unfortunate, because my only copy was loaned to someone years ago and never returned."

Ellen kept her eyes from moving to the spot on the bookshelf where she had touched the bound copy of the thesis only a few months before.

"I am sorry, Ted. What a loss that your thesis has disappeared."

After several minutes of conversation, Ellen gathered her purse and gloves. "I need to be getting back to work, Ted, but could I just trouble you for a glass of water before I go?"

The moment Ted left the room, Ellen moved quickly to the bookshelf. The place where she had seen the thesis at the end of the shelf was vacant, and the space where it had been was now filled by the doctoral dissertation, having fallen over on its side.

At the sound of Ted's returning footsteps, Ellen turned and moved away from the book shelf toward the door. "Here you are, Ellen," he said, handing her a glass of water. Once again, the same false note of camaraderie, but this time Ellen knew that she was not imagining things. Ted had removed the thesis from his shelf, and he was lying about its location. All she wanted to do at the moment was to get out of this house, and fast.

* * *

"I still find it difficult to believe that Ted is a murderer, but something is going on that is very strange." Ellen sipped the cup of tea that Mark had ordered for her in the student cafeteria.

"One thing is certain. I need to locate as many of those theses as possible, and fast. For some reason they seem to be getting hard to find." Mark stirred his coffee and reached across to touch Ellen's hand. "I never should have let you go in there alone."

"Neither one of us had any reason to think that Ted had any part in this," Ellen replied, touched at his concern. "I thought that it would be a simple matter to get the copy of his thesis I had seen. I must say, he was acting strangely from the time I arrived."

"Did he seem threatening to you, in any way?" Mark asked, his eyes narrowing.

"Not threatening—just on guard and somehow defensive. You know, Mark, I have known these people for years, since they were young men, and now I feel that they are potentially dangerous strangers. I don't like this feeling at all."

* * *

The next day, Mark rang the bell at the home of Frank and Anne Gruver. He had talked with Anne earlier in the day and asked if he could see her and Frank as soon as possible. Over the phone, he had explained that he was looking for a copy of Frank's master's thesis as a part of the murder investigation. To his surprise, Anne had told him that Frank had never finished his thesis. They had left Charlottesville before he had completed his research. However, she did know where the folder with all the materials that he had collected from his research had been filed, and she was sure that Frank would agree to his having them.

The expressions on the faces of Frank and Anne, as he came into the living room, told Mark that something was wrong.

Frank was a balding, slightly overweight man, who looked more like an accountant than a successful real estate broker. But his eyes were honest and kind, and people trusted Frank to tell them the truth. At the moment, those eyes were full of concern.

"Mark, when I looked in the filing cabinet upstairs where those materials have always been kept, they were gone." The distress in Anne's voice was obvious.

"I haven't looked at any of that material in years," Frank added. "Actually, I'd probably have thrown it away long ago, but Anne has always taken care of it. She hopes that some day I'll do something with it."

"Where did you have it stored?" Mark asked, taking a seat across from the two of them.

"There is a large filing cabinet in the attic where I keep a number of papers and documents that are not needed on a regular basis. Frank's research papers take up almost a full drawer of the cabinet," Anne explained. "Someone would have had to have carried them away in a box or a large case," Anne explained, "and nothing else in the cabinet seems to have been disturbed."

"Do you know when you last saw the papers?" Mark inquired.

"I haven't really looked in over a year, since I cleaned out the cabinet and threw away quite a bit of duplicate material. I haven't had any reason to open that drawer since." Anne twisted the handkerchief she was holding in her lap.

"Who would have knowledge of where such material would be stored?" Mark asked, knowing full well that only someone very familiar with the house would have access to the attic.

"As far as I know, Mark, no one has broken into the house. I can't remember if I ever mentioned to anyone where those particular papers were stored, but I suppose most of the family knows about the filing cabinet in the attic." The strain in Anne's voice as she said the word *family* was noted by Mark.

"Do you have any idea who might have been into the cabinet?"

Anne started to answer, but Frank interrupted her. "Mark,

clearly this has to be someone very close to us for the papers to have been removed without our suspecting anything. I don't know how we can find out who did this, but we will try."

"That's all I can ask of you, right now." Mark could see how upset each of them was and decided not to prolong the visit. "Please let me know as soon as you have any information," Mark said, as Frank walked with him to the door, leaving a dejected Anne leaning back against the sofa, her hand over her eyes.

CHAPTER TWENTY-ONE

Had the letter been deposited within the range of their search, these fellows would, beyond a question, have found it.
—Poe's "The Purloined Letter"

Mark's next visit was to the office of John Grieco, a man he had only met a few times before interviewing him regarding Henry Dodson, but whom he had seen on television many times. He had agreed to see Mark "between appointments" and Mark arrived fifteen minutes early. The young woman behind the desk greeted him with a trained smile and motioned him toward one of the expensive leather chairs in the waiting room. Mark thought that the decor of the room, with tasteful prints on the wall and an expensive oriental rug on the floor, reflected the trappings of a very successful man.

John Grieco was an intelligent and effective lawyer, who could be a formidable adversary in the courtroom. Those who had a stereotyped impression of fundamentalist Christians as simple or unsophisticated were surprised to find John Grieco both urbane and charming.

The only indication of John Grieco's special "calling" was an unobtrusive picture of a blond, blue-eyed Christ with a halo engulfing the forehead. Mark remembered the picture from Sunday school and wondered how the rugged Jewish carpenter he imagined would have reacted to such an ethereal portrayal. Before he had time to formulate an answer, John Grieco emerged from his office, hands outstretched in greeting. He was an impressive figure in his expensive, well-tailored suit and perfectly matched shirt and tie. His hair was fashionably trimmed and his rugged features carefully shaved. The smile was ingratiating, but it was not reflected in his eyes.

"What can I do for the University's finest this afternoon? I thought we had covered all of the information about poor Henry Dodson when I was in your office." His voice was resonant and his speech carefully trained. Mark had heard it often on the news, as he delivered one of his well-modulated diatribes regarding moral corruption in the Commonwealth.

Mark followed Grieco into his office, which, like the waiting room, was tastefully and expensively decorated. On the elegant mahogany desk was a picture of Grieco's wife and two children. It was for the sake of these children, he often intoned, and for all children, that he had served on the school board before running for the legislature. He had been a powerful advocate for what he termed "school reform," but which his opponents termed "destructive meddling."

"I won't take too much of your time. You must be very busy with the election coming up. I just wanted to ask you for a copy of your master's thesis, if that would be possible."

"Well, whatever for? There certainly has not been a run on my scholarly work in the past." John Grieco seated himself behind his desk and peered at Mark over his reading glasses.

"We are looking for copies of the theses of the group of men who were a part of the secret society to help us in the murder investigation of the young man found in the Poe room. It's possible that there may be some clue in the theses, if we can locate them." Mark tried to keep his voice as noncommittal as possible.

"Have you tried the library?" John Grieco asked. "That would seem to be the most obvious place."

"Yes, we have, but all of the copies have been lost, misplaced, or, perhaps, stolen."

At the word *stolen*, Grieco's eyebrows raised. "Mark, I'm afraid that I haven't seen a copy of my thesis in years. My work with my law practice and my commitment to serving the Lord through public service has taken all of my interest. My study of Edgar Allan Poe seems to belong to some other person and some other time."

"Well, then, I won't bother you any further." Mark stood up to leave. "If, by any chance, you should locate any of your notes pertaining to your research, I would appreciate it if you would call me."

"I most certainly will do that, Mark." Grieco walked with Mark to the door of the office. "Please let me know if there is any way in which I can be of help."

CHAPTER TWENTY-TWO

Will you be so good as to send me a copy of the Historiae of Tacitus—it is a small volume—also some more soap—

Letter of Edgar Allan Poe, May 1826

Ellen and Fannie had decided in advance on bagels and low-fat cream cheese for the Saturday morning treat, after a long discussion about the evils of cholesterol. Then, Fannie had arrived with hot croissants stuffed with eggs, cheese, and bacon. After a few moments of protestations, Ellen bit into hers with pleasure, while Fannie poured them both steaming mugs of coffee.

"Why does this taste so good, when I know that it is loaded with fat and calories?" Ellen just managed to get off the sentence before taking another bite. "Here, try some of these strawberry preserves on it. We might as well go all the way and load up on sugar, as well."

"Don't worry about it. You will be out walking before long in this cold wind and burn off those calories. Now, I intend to go home and put up my feet and just let those calories settle on these beautiful, big hips." Fannie stretched out and put her feet up on the hassock.

"Has anything happened that would help to break the case?" Fannie motioned toward the patrol car outside. "I have to admit, it kind of gives me the creeps to have them hanging around. I feel like a character in one of those old Joan Crawford movies—only you need a long cigarette holder and a real slinky dress for your part, Ellen"

"Speaking of slinky dresses," Ellen said, "I almost forgot the most unusual development. A young woman who has been studying abroad for the past year returned to school a few weeks ago and heard about the murder. She came in to talk with Mark because it seems that she saw someone flashing a light into the Poe room the night of the murder, but she thought it was just some tourist trying to see into the room in the dark," Ellen said.

"Well, that must be your man." Fannie leaned forward excitedly. "What did he look like?"

"*He* had long brown hair and was wearing pumps. She said that it was a woman—a tall woman."

* * *

Mark called Ellen the day the book arrived from Boston to go together to the library. He warned her not to say anything about what they were looking for in front of anyone, since information seemed to escape from the library like pages in a windstorm. "I don't think there is anything malicious going on. It is just that librarians talk among themselves, and they talk to their friends. And you know how fast word travels in this town."

They took the book downstairs to a private reading room and opened it to the introduction. "What we are looking for must either be in the preface or in the footnotes. If this was just about Poe's writing, any book of his collected work would be satisfactory," Ellen observed.

Mark thought for several moments. "You've given me a place to start, Ellen. We need to have someone go through this edition carefully and compare the section in this text to what was removed from the book in the library."

Ellen turned the pages carefully. "I've a young friend just finishing her dissertation in American literature. She'd probably welcome the opportunity to make the comparison. Plus, she owes me a favor."

Ellen turned the book over in her hands, enjoying once again the old book smell that rose from the pages. "What's the secret hiding in these pages, I wonder?" Ellen said, handing the book back to Mark.

"A secret that may have caused someone to murder twice and

may cause that person to murder again," Mark said, giving Ellen a frown. "We have questioned all the people who have worked in the rare books room in the past two years. One of them remembered a young man with red hair asking for the Poe book last spring. He was able to identify a picture of Charlie. The only other person that anyone can remember was a woman who came in late one evening, just before the library closed, and asked to see the book." Mark stood up and stretched. "This could be the same woman that was seen outside the Poe room. We may be dealing with more than one person in all of this, or the murderer may be a woman."

Ellen thought for a few moments and then said, "You know, Mark, I don't think the stalker in the library was a woman. For some reason, I feel that it was a man. Perhaps it was because the shoes sounded heavy—like a man's shoes. Of course, I may be mistaken. I didn't see the person."

Mark and Ellen left the library and walked to the student cafeteria, where they found a table in a corner and compared notes.

"Something is very strange about the manner in which these theses have suddenly disappeared. I know that I saw Ted's only a few months ago, and I can't believe that all the others have vanished." Ellen said.

"Not only the copies of those who live here in Charlottesville, but those of the two men who lived away from here, are missing." Mark took a small notebook from his pocket, flipped it open, and said, "Judge Blake's response was, 'It is very strange that my copy has been misplaced. Perhaps my late wife gave it to one of our children.' Although, I must say, he had a very embarrassed tone in his voice and seemed anxious to get off of the phone. I spoke to Anthony Antonetti's widow, and she was very vague on the subject. She said that all of her husband's papers were in storage and difficult to access. I had the distinct impression that she wished to avoid any further conversation with me." Mark tucked the notebook back in his pocket and stirred his coffee thoughtfully.

"Why would they all suddenly be so evasive about these masters' theses? They surely know this is important."

"Something must seem more important to them than this case. My guess is it has to do with self-interest, but that may be difficult to discover." Mark paid for their coffee. He helped Ellen with her coat, tucked her scarf around her neck, and they walked out into the cold. She had not realized how much she had missed these small attentions.

CHAPTER TWENTY-THREE

The highest hope of pride and power,
I feel hath flown . . .

—Poe's "The Happiest Day"

Mark had been unsuccessful in tracking down the identity of the woman with the flashlight. He interviewed Alice Fenton, the student who had seen the woman at the Poe room. She could only remember that the person was tall, had long hair, and wore low-heeled pumps. The woman apparently was wearing a raincoat or a long jacket over a dark skirt, because Eileen did not notice anything about the clothing. "It was dark and I just didn't think it was important." Eileen twisted a pencil nervously as she spoke.

Mark had asked Jake to join him for the interview, and he patted the young woman on the shoulder protectively. "It's OK. We just appreciate that you called to let us know about this. A lot of people would not have bothered to get involved."

"Did the person give any indication that she saw you?" Mark asked.

"I don't think so. I came out of my friend's room in the next colonnade from the Poe room. She was graduating, and I'd stayed over to attend the graduation ceremonies. I went into my room. It's just five doorways up from the Poe room. I paused for a moment, when I saw the person at the Poe room, and then I went into my room. I had left my door open to get some air, so there was no sound of my door being opened or closed. Besides, the woman was staring intently into the room, so I don't think she noticed me. It gave me kind of a creepy feeling, so I really didn't want her to notice me."

"You said that she was tall. Was she heavyset?" Mark asked.

"Well, not fat, I don't think, but—uh—sturdy. I noticed that her hands were fairly large."

"Was she wearing any rings, or a bracelet?" Jake asked, glancing at Mark, who was taking notes as they questioned the student.

"I don't remember any jewelry. The flashlight was long and black, like the kind people carry in the trunk of their cars in case of an emergency. I'm sorry I can't remember anything more useful. I really liked Charlie Allan, although I did not know him well," she added, shaking her head"

The young woman gathered her belongings and was about to leave when she hesitated at the door and turned back to Mark and Jake. "I don't know if I should mention this. It's probably just gossip, but the past few months before he died, Charlie may have been involved with someone. Several times I saw a woman coming out of his room wearing dark glasses and a scarf."

"Do you think it was the same woman you saw at the Poe room the night of the murder?" The excitement in Mark's voice at this new development was evident.

"I don't think so," Alice replied. "The woman at the Poe room seemed taller and heavier, but then I can't be certain."

"Do you have any idea who the woman coming out of Charlie's room might have been?" Jake asked.

Alice was visibly upset at continuing the discussion. She took a deep breath and said quietly, "I didn't recognize the person, but a friend of mine told me that he saw Charlie and a woman in a bar in Washington recently and he recognized the woman. It was Mrs. Mitchell, the dean's wife."

After Alice left, Mark and Jake sat for a few moments without saying anything. Finally, Jake broke the silence. "Well, what do you make of that, Mark?"

Mark shook his head. "It could be a rumor. Students love to make up such stories about professors and their wives—particularly a wife as colorful as Rebecca Mitchell. It could also be a case of mistaken identity. Or, it could be that Charlie Allan and Rebecca Mitchell were having an affair. I gather it would not be the first time that Mrs. Mitchell was supposedly involved with someone other than her husband . . . and someone a lot younger."

"Do you think she could have been the woman outside the door that night?" Jake was turning the pages of his notepad. "I never met the lady, so I have no idea what she looks like."

"She is tall, very thin, and she has blonde hair. She doesn't seem to fit the description of the person Alice saw." Mark was silent for a few moments and then he continued, "Could this just be a coincidence, or did the killer have a woman working with him who was outside the Poe room on the night of the murder? After all, we know that a woman was in the rare book room looking at the damaged book."

"Yeah, if only the young man working in the library that night could remember more about her. He seemed to have been paying more attention to his girl friend, who was waiting for him, than to the woman who asked for the book." Jake stood up and put on his coat. "All he remembered was that she was fairly tall, wore a funny hat pulled down, almost covering her eyes, and she had a husky voice. That doesn't give us a lot to go on."

But there was one other possibility that had not yet occurred to Mark or to Jake.

CHAPTER TWENTY-FOUR

The victor began to bite his opponent viciously and where many students carried guns and knives for protection.

Letter of Edgar Allan Poe

"Whoever said that it has to be a woman? I know men who like to get dressed up in women's clothes and parade around." Fannie was putting away the remains of their morning's feast and wrapping half of the coffee cake to take home in her purse.

"I haven't heard of anything like that around here," Ellen said, looking at her friend doubtfully.

"Hah! If you cleaned as many houses as I have over the years, you would know about those pink nighties tucked in with the jockey shorts and the high-heeled shoes way in the back of the closet behind *his* tennis shoes. There are men who get their kicks dressing up in women's clothing, and some of them go all the way and venture outside, if they are pretty sure not to be recognized. I remember one old goat had about five long wigs stashed in a special cabinet over his work bench. Who would have guessed, since he was as bald as a picked chicken."

"It would explain a lot," Ellen said thoughtfully. "Mark said it was a large woman and there was no jewelry that the student could remember. Fannie, just how well does the grapevine work among your friends? Do they share information about finding—uh—strange articles of clothing when they are cleaning?"

"Well, there isn't anything to keep me from 'priming the pump' a little. I'll ask some folks, just casually, if they have noticed anything interesting along that line lately. I just wish I could come across a little black pair of panties or a lace brassiere in the mayor's closet, one of these days," Fannie said, with a mischievous grin. "Even better, I sure would like to catch him strutting around in three-inch pumps with those bandy legs of his. On second thought," Fannie said, making a face, "I don't think I want to see that sight after all." They both laughed.

* * *

When Ellen shared Fannie's hypothesis with Mark, he looked thoughtful. "I guess it is possible. We sure haven't been able to come up with any suspects among the women involved in this case that fit the description. It is just hard for me to imagine a cross-dresser wandering around Charlottesville. Or, perhaps he just dressed this way when he needed to move around the grounds or the library without being recognized."

"From some of the things that Fannie tells me, it isn't hard to imagine just about anything happening in Charlottesville."

Ellen smiled to herself, as she thought of how this case had altered her naive and provincial attitudes about her hometown. There had always been scandals and colorful occurrences in Charlottesville. She simply had led a life that was protected from much of it. According to popular legend, the student-run honor system for which the University was famous grew out of an altercation between a student and a faculty member in the 19th century which had resulted in the faculty member being shot to death on the Lawn. The students and faculty established the honor system to control such behavior. Violence was not new to the Grounds. Edgar Allen Poe had described in a letter seeing a situation outside his door where "the victor began to bite his opponent viciously and where many students carried guns and knives for protection."

"Mark, I have asked Fannie to do a little investigative work for us. Oh, nothing dangerous," she added, in response to his look of alarm. "Just to ask a few people—her friends and family—who have some inside information about possible aberrant behaviors regarding dress that they might notice. It is amazing what a cleaning person notices when they are poking that dust mop around in the closets and under the beds."

Mark grinned. "I know one thing. I sure am glad that I have never had enough money to afford a cleaning lady."

"Just don't ask and I won't need to tell you where she gets her information. You never know what might be helpful," Ellen laughed.

"Oh, another thing—the young woman you sent to me regarding the Poe books has finished her work and she found nothing unusual in the introductory material." Mark walked over to the window and watched the cars speeding by on Route 250, thankful that he was not in charge of enforcing local traffic laws. "She acknowledged, however, that she's not an expert on Poe, so she may have missed something."

"The expert on Poe that would be most helpful to us is Ted. Unfortunately, he isn't the best person to ask about this particular work right now," Ellen said.

* * *

Fannie called Ellen at work the next week—an unusual occurrence—and Ellen was concerned when she heard her friend's voice in the middle of a weekday. "What's the matter, Fannie?" she asked.

"Don't get upset. I'm fine, but I just heard some news that I thought you would like to hear, as well."

"Hold on just a minute, Fannie." Ellen walked over and shut the door to her office. "What is it?"

"It is Etta's day to clean the Mitchells' house and she found something very interesting. Rebecca Mitchell has about six wigs stored on a shelf in her closet in hat boxes. They're different colors—and styles. Apparently she picks her hair depending on where she's visiting and what she's doing." Ellen could hear the critical note in Fannie's voice, but decided not to comment.

"She and Ted Mitchell are about the same size. She wears a size 10 woman's shoe and he wears a size 8 man's. They are also about the same height. He could have dressed in his wife's clothes and worn one of her wigs that night."

"For that matter, Rebecca could have worn one of the wigs and disguised herself," said Ellen. "I'll share this with Mark and thanks, Fannie. I really appreciate your help. See you on Saturday."

* * *

Mark was intrigued with the information about the wigs, but he could see no way to make use of it. "We don't have enough evidence against Ted to go into the house with a search warrant, and there's no law against people having wigs in their closets."

"The more this goes on, the more it seems that every person who is involved could have been guilty. I'm certain that there is some clue to all of this in that library book, if only there was someone we could trust to help us find it. Without a copy of any of the theses, we have no idea what might be related to the book in the library."

"I had the feeling that Anne knew who had removed the notes from their attic, but that she couldn't say. I'm going to have to question her again, soon."

Ellen decided not to mention to Mark her discussion with Reverend Evans. She wasn't sure how much she could tell him without betraying a confidence, and she would rather that Anne came to that conclusion on her own and told Mark. Surely, she thought to herself, Reverend Evans' involvement in the situation was based solely on his desire to protect his daughter.

CHAPTER TWENTY-FIVE

There are moments when, even to the sober eye of Reason, the world of our sad Humanity may assume the semblance of a hell . . .
—Poe's "The Premature Burial"

If Ellen was not telling Mark everything she knew about Reverend Evans, Mark had not told Ellen about the possible involvement between Rebecca Mitchell and Charlie. Like Ellen, he had made a decision that this information should not be shared with anyone unless it was necessary to the case. He made an appointment to see Rebecca at a time when her husband would be out of the house, and she would be alone.

When he arrived at the Mitchell pavilion, Rebecca met him at the door wearing an elegant dressing gown and waving a cigarette in a long, jeweled holder. Her hair was immaculately coiffed, her make-up applied expertly, and she wore a few pieces of tasteful and expensive jewelry. Mark thought that she certainly looked the part of a wealthy sophisticate who might take her pleasure wherever she chose.

She swept before him into the parlor, as she referred to it, and arranged herself artfully on a velvet sofa in what seemed to Mark to be a deliberate pose. He was reminded of Bette Davis in one of those movies from the 40's. Everything about this woman seemed somehow to be contrived. It was as though there was a persona applied very artfully over the original that prevented any possibility of making a connection to the real person within. He wondered what she might really be like when she wasn't playing this role, or had she played it so long that she really had become this person.

His dad had told him that when the Mitchells were first married, she was a skinny, red-haired girl with buck teeth, and most people intimated that all Ted saw in the homely Rebecca was family money and position. Rebecca came from an old Virginia family, while Ted was the son of a dockworker in Norfolk. Both shared a love for riding and often came to the stables where Mark's father worked.

For some years, they had seemed to be happy together. Rebecca hosted the incessant parties and receptions that were a part of Ted's rise through the academic ranks. She courted the approval of department chairs and deans and was an active member of faculty wives, where she made certain to serve on the committees that brought her into contact with the wives of those men who could be most helpful to her husband's career. All the time, she seemed to epitomize the loyal help-mate, ever willing to bask in the reflected light of her husband's success.

When Ted finally made it and was appointed dean of the college, Rebecca began to emerge from her chrysalis. She had her teeth straightened. There were shopping trips to New York for clothes. A designer from Washington helped her to make over the pavilion when they moved onto the Lawn—turning his nose up at most of the eighteenth-century antiques offered by the University and preferring French provincial, which he maintained Jefferson would have preferred.

Ted also changed from the slightly rumpled academic into the elegant Dean. His spectacles were replaced by contacts and his tweeds by Italian silk. He drove a silver BMW, and she had a Mercedes convertible. They gave dinner parties at the country club, and they flew to the Islands in January. They had become a part of the "beautiful people," and the movie stars and millionaires who lived in Albemarle County on their fancy horse farms included them in their events. They rode to the hounds with the members of the Hunt Club. She was president of the Arts Council, and he served on the board of the Philanthropy Trust. They had made it.

Then the relationship between them began to change. The two stopped going to parties together, with one or the other begging off because of illness or travel. They took separate vacations and then moved into separate bedrooms. She inherited money and an apartment in New York, where she lived most of the year. She was rumored to have had an affair with a famous sports figure in New York. Ted's name was linked to a number of women—one widow in particular—but he was always very discreet.

Periodically, however, they would appear at the faculty club—she in a Paris gown and a diamond necklace, holding onto her husband's elegant arm as though they had never been apart.

"What is it you wanted to ask me about, Mark?" She was smiling, but her eyes were wary. "You sounded so official on the phone."

"Some students have reported to us that you were having a relationship with Charlie Allan. I want to know if that is the truth." Mark had decided that the direct approach would be best. He could not hope to win any cat and mouse games with a professional like Rebecca.

"My, you do believe in getting right to the point don't you? Surely, you must know that students make up a lot of things about their professors. They seem to find me exceptionally interesting for some reason." She took a long drag on the cigarette and blew the smoke in a haze above her head.

"I thought the same thing," Mark said, "but I had to ask you. This could be important to finding out why Charlie was murdered. If you know anything about him, you need to tell me."

She got up slowly from the sofa and moved to the window. She stood looking out at the Lawn for several minutes, and Mark saw that her shoulders were shaking. He thought she was laughing, and he felt his hostility rise toward this lacquered mannequin. He was about to stand up and leave the room when she turned towards him, her face streaked with tears.

"I used to walk over to the Corner sometimes late at night for a drink when I was alone in the house. You know that Ted is seldom here when I'm in town." Rebecca turned away from the window and came back to sit on the sofa. The pose was gone. She put out the cigarette and placed the holder on the table.

Mark sat in the chair facing her. He was amazed at the transformation that had taken place. The woman across from him looked older and very tired. She leaned back against the cushions without artifice and rubbed her hands across her face, ignoring the mascara that made dark circles under her eyes.

"At first, we just chatted in the bar. He was a very nice young man. When he asked me about that box, I invited him to our pavilion for a drink and to show him some of the pictures of Ted and the group of students in that secret society. He was fascinated by them and by the stories I could tell him about Virginia and about the University. We were friends, Mark, that's all. I went to his room to see the papers he had found. We talked and had a little wine together."

"Did he tell you anything about his investigation into the secret society?" Mark asked.

"Only that he was talking to a number of people and that one person in particular had been very helpful to him. He wouldn't tell me who it was because he said that the whole point of a secret society was that it was *secret*. He was really intrigued by the mystery of it all and mentioned the possibility of starting the society again with the help of the old members. I warned him one time about getting too involved. Ted always spoke about that group reluctantly, as though it made him uneasy to have been a part of it—as though he didn't want to discuss it."

"What about the trip to Washington? You were seen there with Charlie Allan."

"I invited him to go to a play with me at the Kennedy Center. He had never been there, and he was like a big kid looking at the red carpeting and the crystal chandeliers."

"Does Ted know about your relationship with Charlie, Rebecca?" Mark asked.

"I don't know. If he did, he probably wouldn't care," she went on. "He'd be more surprised if I told him Charlie and I were just friends. We've gotten very proficient at hurting each other."

"Why do you stay together if there is so little left to your marriage?" Mark realized this was not necessarily a routine inquiry, but he could not resist trying to understand this strange relationship. "I'm sorry to be so inquisitive, but I need to understand what was going on."

"There has always been something about you, Mark, that I feel I can trust. Well—here goes. I think that Ted and I are each afraid to let the other go. It is as though we are a part of the persona created by the other. Believe it or not, once in a while we actually care for each other. There are times when we talk, we dance, we even make love. But it never lasts. I go back to my New York friends, and he goes back to his career and his other women."

"How did Charlie fit into this picture?" Mark asked, wanting to get the conversation back to Charlie from this embarrassing inquiry.

"He was just a special friend—almost a son. Charlie really was a big kid. I think that is what got him into trouble. When I heard about him being killed, I was devastated. I still am, Mark." She paused, "But life does go on."

Rebecca leaned over and placed a new cigarette from the dish on the table into the holder. She took a compact from her pocket and repaired the damage to her face. Then she offered the lighter to Mark. "Would you light my cigarette, please?" The Rebecca who had met him at the door was back. She blew a puff of smoke that enveloped her face as she leaned back against the cushions.

"Do you mind seeing yourself out, Mark? I think that I will sit here for a while." The diamonds gleamed on her fingers as she waved him towards the door.

Mark walked away from the pavilion, amazed at the misery people could inflict upon each other. Had Charlie somehow become caught in this web of artifice and betrayal?

CHAPTER TWENTY-SIX

. . . An established name is an estate in tenure, or a throne in possession.

—Poe's 1831 Letter to Mr. B

Fannie was early on Saturday, and Ellen could tell from the expression on her face that she had something very important to share. As soon as they were seated by the fire and the scones Ellen had bought at the farmer's market were buttered and jammed, Fannie began.

"Hold on to your hat for this one, because even I couldn't believe what I was hearing. You know, I'd asked several of my relatives and close friends for information on unusual behaviors, like we planned. Well, my cousin Tom came over last night and we were sitting there talking, when all of a sudden he looked at me with this real serious expression on his face. He said he needed to tell me something, but that he could not be involved in any way, and if he was asked about this, he'd deny on a stack of bibles it ever happened."

Ellen put her cup on the table. "What could be so damaging that he's afraid he will be questioned about it? Did he see something the night of the murder? Does he work for the University?" Ellen frowned.

"No, not now. He's retired." Fannie leaned forward. "Tom worked at the country club for thirty years. He was the night watchman and did some of the maintenance on the grounds. I had mentioned to Tom that Anne and Reverend Evans were involved in the investigation."

Ellen opened her eyes wide, as if to protest, and Fannie interrupted her before she could speak.

"I didn't tell them any of the details—just that Miss Anne had known the first victim and that Reverend Evans and the sheriff were anxious that she not be involved in all of this. I also told them that the man who was murdered years ago was a blackmailer who had threatened a number of people with exposure."

"Well, what did Tom know that could possibly have anything to do with this case?" Ellen asked.

"Tom doesn't miss much, and believe me he saw a'plenty around that country club in the late evenings. He was there when the pool closed and when the parties broke up, so he knew a lot; but he kept his mouth shut. He told me that late at night the pool used to be a meeting place for some of the gay members of the community, who are still locked up tight in their closets. They came to have a late night swim and then meet in the locker room and the showers. Of course, they didn't know anyone saw them or knew what they were doing, and Tom was careful that they didn't notice him or, if they did, they'd assume he didn't know what was going on. If you think Etta's act with Ted Mitchell was right out of 'Step n' Fetchit,' Tom's act at the country club was from the best of 'Amos and Andy.' He called them all 'governor' and slapped his thigh and rolled his eyes."

"I think this is something else that I really wish I didn't have to know," Ellen sighed. "What connection did these late night meetings in the pool at the country club have to do with the murders in the Poe room?"

"I can't think of any easy way to tell you this, so I'll just say it. Two of the people who were involved in those late night meetings were Bowman Ward and Reverend Evans."

Ellen sank back in her chair and felt the air rush out of her lungs. The connection was immediately obvious to her, as it had been to Tom. If blackmail were involved, these two men were prime candidates, particularly if there was a link through Anne to the blackmailer.

"I just can't believe this is true, Fannie. I have known both of these men all of my adult life. How could they have kept a secret like this?"

"My guess is that those who are closest to them might have been suspicious, but chose not to admit the truth, even to themselves. I'm sure they were very, very careful—and, who knows, maybe they ended the relationship entirely years ago. Tom also remembered the Dodson boy. He came out to the club fairly often with some friend of his who was a member. It's very possible that Henry Dodson found out what was going on and made use of it."

"I don't know what to do with this information. Tom will deny it, if anyone questions him, and if this has no relevance to the case, I don't want to be the one to make this public." Ellen twisted the napkin in her hand into several small knots. "What am I going to do?"

Fannie leaned over and pressed her friend's hand. "I think that right now you should do what Tom and a lot of my folks have always done. Put this information away and don't do anything with it, unless it becomes absolutely necessary. There is no point in stirring up a hornet's nest, as long as the hornets aren't doing any harm. Hey, the connection to the book still seems to be the strongest lead. Why don't you see where that goes, first."

CHAPTER TWENTY-SEVEN

Till secrecy shall Knowledge be in the environs of Heaven.
—Poe's "Al Aaraaf"

Several days later, Mark went to visit with Anne Gruver again. This time, Frank was at work and the two of them were alone. She had made coffee and they were sitting in the sun room of the comfortable old house on Park Street.

"I have thought about this many times, and I don't know why those papers were disturbed," Anne said. But Mark could tell from the way in which she spoke that Anne *did* have some idea what had happened.

"It seems to me that it must have been someone in your family or someone who is inside the house on a regular basis," Mark said. "Is there a cleaning person or a gardener, for instance, who has access to the house?"

Anne shook her head. "I haven't had any regular help for several years, since the children left home. I enjoy taking care of things myself. I do have a person who helps with the garden from time to time, but he never comes into the house. Twice a year, I have a cleaning service come in and do the windows and floors, but they haven't been here for several months."

"Are you afraid that it was Frank who took the papers, Mrs. Gruver?" Mark could think of no easy way to ask the question.

"No," she replied in a low voice. "I don't think it was Frank. I think it may have been my father. He is so concerned that all of this may be made public that he is trying to protect me in any way that he can."

"Have you asked him?" Mark tried to keep the surprise out of his voice. He knew that her father was an Episcopal priest and he couldn't imagine him committing this act.

"Yes, and he denies everything. If he took the papers, he may have destroyed them. I am only telling you this because I don't want you to focus on Frank. He has been through enough."

"But what is your father afraid of? This investigation doesn't necessarily involve your family." Mark was puzzled by the intensity of Anne's concern.

"I haven't told anyone but Ellen, Mark, outside of our family, of course. I asked her to keep my confidence until I was ready to tell you—and now I am ready. Henry Dodson was the father of my daughter, Sarah. Frank and Sarah and I have searched for Henry for several years, because my Emily wanted to make contact with her father. Now, of course, we know that he was murdered. It is this connection to our family that I believe my father is trying so desperately to keep a secret."

Mark was silent for a few moments, thinking about this new information. He could understand why Ellen had not told him—but then also wondered what other information she was keeping to herself.

"Anne, I can't imagine why this information needs to be made public at this time, although it may help to explain your father's behavior. I'm still not sure why he fears our looking at Frank's thesis."

"I believe that he wants this matter to end before all the facts need to be revealed," Anne said.

Later, when Mark was sharing this conversation with Ellen, he asked her if there were any other secrets she needed to share with him. Ellen almost blurted out the information about Reverend Evans and Bowman Ward, but she could not. Something kept her from breaking her silence. Instead, she said, "Mark, just as Anne said, I think Reverend Evans was mistakenly trying to protect someone he loved." Ellen, was thinking to herself, the loved one he is trying to protect, however, may not be his daughter.

Ellen felt burdened by the information she possessed regarding Reverend Evans and his relationship with the vice chancellor. Sometime soon, she was going to have to tell Mark everything, and she dreaded that moment. Secrets told in confidence and actions observed in the dark of night would cause irreparable pain if they had to be revealed and dragged into the glaring light of day, and it would be partly her fault.

CHAPTER TWENTY-EIGHT

Ah, distinctly I remember it was in the bleak December;
—*Poe's "The Raven"*

Weeks went by, and still there had been no new breaks in the case. Ellen and Fannie were eating Christmas cookies and drinking hot cider. Rays from a watery sun were turning the ice on the branches to shimmering crystals.

"It's really beautiful out there this morning, but not a good day for walking or driving. How in the world did you get in from the country with all the ice?" Ellen was standing at the window admiring the wintry pageant.

"It wasn't too bad after I got on I-64. Slipping and sliding was better than sitting in a cold trailer. My electricity went off again this morning."

"You know you can always stay here. There is an empty bed upstairs for you." Ellen worried about Fannie alone in the trailer during the winter.

"I know and, if it gets too bad, I'll be on your front door step with all my worldly possessions. But you know how foolish I am about my home. I love that place because it is mine and it's paid for and, if I do say so myself, it looks pretty good. And by the way, my friend, if you could only drive, you'd have a car and be out there to see me more often."

Fannie had brought up a subject that caused frequent heated discussions between the two old friends. Ellen had never learned to drive, and she had never owned a car. As the years went by, she had gotten used to the situation.

"Don't start playing that old record. I would be a danger to anyone on the road."

Fannie snorted, "The danger is that you can't get yourself around. You have good vision, your health is excellent, you could afford an inexpensive car, and there is no good reason why you shouldn't get into the 20th century now that it is the 21st."

Ellen wanted to change the subject. "How did that slipcover you were making come out?"

"It looks great. Those drapes the mayor's wife was discarding had just enough material to cover the chair and make a pillow for the sofa." Fannie had decorated her trailer with discards and throwaways with great imagination. Plants, abandoned by fashionable garden club members, bloomed and blossomed in every window. Chairs destined for the trash heap had been painted bright colors. A sofa with a broken spring had been repaired and covered with a quilt made of patches of wool and velvet, carefully saved and sewn together. "The place is looking pretty good—and it's mine! Here, have another one of these sugar cookies."

"Oh, I have had too many already," Ellen said, reaching for another.

"Don't worry. There's nothing in them to hurt you. They are mostly just butter and sugar." Fannie laughed at her friend's look of dismay. "Besides, it's almost Christmas, and you need to do a little celebrating. Where's your tree?"

"I haven't felt like celebrating this year, Fannie. This whole business with the murders has gotten to me. I feel like I'm keeping secrets that I should tell and I feel terrible about it. What I need is for Santa to leave in my stocking a magician who can produce a copy of all these masters' theses—and then connect the introduction in that library book to one of them."

Fannie sat, thoughtfully staring into the fire, until Ellen said, "Hey, are you trying to dream up my magician for me?"

"Maybe I am," Fannie replied. "You know, Etta Mae worked for many years for a professor in the English department who lived on University Circle in one of those big old apartments. I can't remember his name, but I do know that he used a cane because he had trouble walking."

"Oh, you mean Martin Harrison. I think he's dead."

"No, he isn't," Fannie replied emphatically, pleased she knew something Ellen didn't. "Etta Mae still goes there once in a while to clean up the apartment when he's going to be in town. He has been staying in New Mexico, near his nephew. He also has an apartment in New York. Once or twice a year, he comes back to Charlottesville to check on things."

"Well, what does he have to do with my magician?"

"Etta Mae says that his apartment is filled with wonderful antiques, beautiful paintings, and old, beat-up filing cabinets. He told her that he kept many of the papers and writings of his students and that it's hard for him to get rid of them. He said they are his connection to his 'professorial past,' or something like that. He also told her how fond he was of your husband."

"Good heavens!" Ellen leaned forward eagerly. "I think that Martin taught some American literature courses when my husband was chairman of the department. Is it possible that he could have some papers from those years?"

"It can't hurt to ask. He'd probably be pleased to hear from you. Pass me those cookies, please, and let's get back to the subject of automobiles."

* * *

After Fannie had gone home, Ellen looked up Martin Harrison in the phone book and, to her surprise, found that he still had a phone listed on University Circle. When she dialed the listing, she got a recording that gave her a number in New Mexico. That number was answered by a woman, who told her that Professor Harrison was planning to visit Charlottesville in a few days, after a visit in New York, where he was moving out of his apartment there. Mr. Harrison and his nephew intended to clean out Professor Harrison's apartment in Charlottesville and move him permanently to a retirement home in New Mexico.

Ellen hung up and re-dialed Martin Harrison's number in Charlottesville and, this time, she let the machine play past the message about the number in New Mexico, until it came to a place where she could leave a message for him. After identifying herself, she requested that Mr. Harrison call her as soon as he came to town. "This is an extremely urgent matter," she said.

Ellen told Mark of Fannie's latest contribution to the investigation, and he chuckled, "I think that we need to put Fannie on our special investigation team, with all she knows about the folks in this town." Then he looked more thoughtfully at Ellen. "For that matter, maybe we should put both of you on there. You make quite a combo."

"Never mind that," Ellen smiled. "I think you should have someone watch Martin Harrison's apartment and let us know the minute he returns. I don't trust that answering machine. We don't want to take a chance on his destroying or removing those papers before we have spoken with him. Those filing cabinets will probably be the first things to go when they start cleaning out the apartment."

CHAPTER TWENTY-NINE

Unless incidentally it has not concern either with duty or with truth.

—*Poe's "The Poetic"*

As it turned out, Ellen was right. The papers were within hours of going to the trash when Mark was informed by the officer on duty that he had been watching the wrong apartment, and only a chance remark by a neighbor, who noticed the patrol car in the vicinity, led him to the correct address. When the officer reported to Mark that there were boxes stacked on the porch, apparently waiting removal, Mark ordered him to speak to Mr. Harrison at once and ask that nothing be removed until he could get there. Then he called Ellen. "Can you come with me to see Mr. Harrison as soon as possible, Ellen? He knows you, and I think that he will feel more comfortable speaking about this matter if you are there. I'll pick you up in a few minutes."

On the way to University Circle, Ellen recalled the man they were going to see. Unlike so many other faculty members, who seemed intent on getting as far away from the students as possible, Martin Harrison chose to live in the neighborhood near the University and near the students. She remembered him as a sophisticated, urbane man with a sense of humor. His physical disability had apparently kept him from marrying, and his students had become an extended family for him.

They pulled up in front of an aging, but still beautiful, building that Ellen knew contained spacious 19th-century apartments with high ceilings, parquet floors, and fireplaces in each room. Mark pulled the unmarked police car onto the sidewalk. They entered the foyer and located Martin Harrison's name on the bell. After a few moments, they were admitted into the foyer of Martin Harrison's apartment.

"My dear Ellen. It has been many years, but you are as lovely as ever." Martin Harrison was almost bent double with age and the arthritis that had afflicted him from his youth, but the twinkle in his blue eyes was just the same. Ellen remembered that he had flirted with her in a very gentlemanly manner when her husband was chairman of the English department and he was a member of the faculty.

They entered the living room of the apartment, and Ellen noted that the room was beautifully furnished. The high ceilings gave a sense of spaciousness and the dark, red velvet drapes a feeling of warmth.

"Please let me introduce you to my nephew, Arnold Harrison." Arnold shook hands with Mark and bowed to Ellen. Ellen was surprised at how unlike his uncle he was. He was tall and handsome, with eyes that were cool and reserved.

With a distinct trace of annoyance in his voice he said, "I hope this will not take too long. We have a great deal of packing to finish before the movers arrive. And now we are bringing boxes back in that I thought were on the way out."

"Now Arnold, we have plenty of time. Please put some water on for tea for our guests." Martin watched his nephew exit from the room with a small sigh of what Ellen thought was relief.

"I am sorry about that answering machine, but there was only a garbled set of messages on the tape, Ellen."

"It is good to see you again, Martin. It has been a long time, indeed."

"Whatever has brought you bustling to my apartment with the gendarmes this morning? I trust that I have not committed any grievous breach of the law." Martin Harrison moved with difficulty to his chair and eased himself into it.

"No, Martin, you have not committed any crime, but someone has. This is Chief Pace of the University Police. He has been investigating two murders—one committed thirty years ago, when you were a professor, and one committed last spring."

Mark briefly summarized the events leading up to their visit while Professor Harrison looked on in amazement. When he finished, Martin Harrison said, "I remember hearing something about that secret society, but I didn't really think it existed or, if it did, that it would have any special significance. Students at the University have always enjoyed these secret groups full of mumbo jumbo and clandestine night meetings. Mostly they do no harm, and indeed some of them have been very financially supportive of University needs." Martin paused to adjust the pillow behind his back. "You know the Secret Seven Society, whose members always leave their messages at the feet of the Thomas Jefferson statue in the Rotunda. I think they provide major support to the institution."

Arnold returned to the room as they were describing the events of the past year, overhearing some of the conversation.

"What has all of this got to do with my Uncle?" Arnold inquired. "He has lived away from Charlottesville most of the time during the past ten years, and he has not been at all well. I don't want him to be upset."

"Never mind, Arnold. I'm not about to expire from the exertion of speaking to these interesting people. In fact, I rather am enjoying this break from the monotony."

Arnold's disapproval of the situation, and of his uncle's barely veiled innuendo, was evident. "I'm only looking out for your welfare."

"We understand," said Mark, looking right past Arnold at Mr. Harrison, "that you have saved many of the papers written by your students over the years. As I mentioned, all of the masters' theses written by the people involved in the secret society have disappeared. Ellen was stalked in the library by someone when she went in search of them. She found that they had been removed from the shelves and probably destroyed in the library, since they could not have been taken out past the security system."

"What in particular are you looking for, Chief Pace? My memory is still very good, but I haven't looked at most of these files in years. I did not generally keep copies of masters' theses since, as you have said, they were in the library—or should be."

"We have located this library book that we believe was referenced in the note found hidden in the fireplace hearth by the young man who was murdered last year. We believe there's something in this book that is key to the identity of the murderer." Mark handed the book to Mr. Harrison. "It is our assumption that the connection between one of the masters' theses and the book is in the preface."

Martin Harrison took the book and motioned to his nephew to move a floor lamp closer to his chair. "Arnold, please serve our guests tea or coffee while I take a few moments to read this. Just go on about your business. This won't take me very long."

Arnold led them into the tiny kitchen, where a carafe of coffee was already prepared and a pot of tea was brewing under a tea cozy. He motioned toward the table. "Uncle insists on his tea and I prefer coffee, so there is plenty of both. The cups are there on the shelf." He left the room abruptly, leaving them to serve themselves.

They took their coffee and walked leisurely through the rooms. In spite of the stacks of boxes, the apartment was still a pleasure to behold. The walls were hung with a collection of neo-realism paintings that were to go eventually to the University museum. Each painting was carefully lit, to make it stand out from the wall and still blend in with the decor of the rooms. Deep oriental rugs covered the floors, and the furnishings were fine antiques mixed with upholstered chairs and sofas in soft velvets and brocades.

Arnold came up behind them in the hallway. "This place has just become too much for Uncle. When he moves into the retirement home in New Mexico, he won't need to keep up two homes anymore. Besides, travel has become very difficult for him. I wasn't sure that we were going to make this trip. In addition, cleaning out the small apartment in New York was tiring. Fortunately, we were able to sell it, furniture and all. Most of his personal items were moved out some years ago."

The tour of the apartment was suddenly interrupted by a call from the other room. Martin Harrison was sitting with his finger marking the place in the book where he had been reading.

"There is something about this that is familiar to me, but it has been a long time and many students have come and gone in thirty years. I'll need some time to go through my files and someone to help me. Perhaps you could suggest some person."

"But, Uncle, we need to get back to New Mexico as soon as possible. You can't stay in this place all by yourself."

"It is my decision, Arnold. I am not senile and I have no intention of leaving here just now. I suggest that you go back to New Mexico without me."

"But, what about your plans, Uncle Martin? The retirement home won't wait forever for you to make up your mind. It's very difficult to get admitted there."

"Arnold, I hate to tell you this, but I really don't care very much for New Mexico. All that sun is bad for my disposition. I have realized since we came here how much I miss Virginia and Charlottesville and my apartment. I want to stay here for a while. Etta Mae can come in and clean for me, as she used to. I have already spoken to her."

Arnold gaped at his uncle in amazement, and then in fury. "After all that I have done for you and this is how you repay my concern for your best interests. You want to stay here—alone—in this antiquated apartment!"

"Yes, Arnold, that is what I want to do."

"Well, don't expect me to come running out here when you need help." Arnold turned and walked down the hall, his heels tapping angrily against the wooden floors. A door shut at the end of the hall with a resounding bang.

"Arnold means well, but I fear that he is more interested in my money than in my welfare. That retirement home in New Mexico is one of those places that you buy into for a fortune, and then when you die it goes to your estate and can be sold again for a larger fortune. I think that my apartment here fits me comfortably. I really have missed it very much." Martin Harrison looked around the room with affection and patted the arm of his chair. "Very much, indeed."

"Martin, you wouldn't have tricked your nephew into bringing you back under the pretense of closing this place, when you really planned to stay here all of the time, would you?"

"Well, Ellen, I wanted to see how it would be to stay in my home again, and I will tell you it feels just fine. Do you think that I can locate old friends?"

"I know you have already located one of them, Martin." Ellen reached out and took his hand.

Mark interrupted this reunion reluctantly. "We had better be getting back, Ellen. Will you call me as soon as you have had a chance to read the book, sir?"

"Most assuredly, young man. In the meantime, I plan to employ Etta Mae to come in as often as possible and help me begin to rearrange my files. The answer may be in there, if only I can find it."

CHAPTER THIRTY

. . . I have not been as others were—
I have not seen
As others saw . . .

—*Poe's "Alone"*

Mark and Ellen decided to walk the few blocks to the University, and Mark asked one of the police officers to return the police car to headquarters. They crossed the often-painted Beta Bridge over the railroad tracks, which was today a bright red and garish green, advertising a holiday party that took place weeks ago, before the students left for the semester break. Ellen thought that if someone had taken pictures of the graffiti on this bridge over the years, they would have an historical record of the University of Virginia, of both the trivial and the profound. She recalled graphic displays ranging from "Beta Mu Sisters Do it Better" to "Stop the Bombing."

They walked along the tree-lined sidewalks, still littered by refuse from the weekend fraternity parties. Mark kicked at a beer can and muttered something about spoiled brats with nothing better to do than trash the neighborhood. Ellen knew he was worried about something and that it wasn't the slovenly habits of errant youth.

"What's wrong, Mark?" she asked, placing her hand on his arm.

"This is definitely a long shot, Ellen, and we may be involving Martin Harrison needlessly. The more people that become a part of this, the more possibilities for someone to get hurt."

"Mark, are you concerned that I'm still in danger? There have been no further signs from the person in the library."

"Perhaps it was a coincidence that the murderer just happened to be in the library at that time, but I don't think so," Mark replied.

"I'm anxious about you becoming any more involved in this than you already are. I probably should not have asked you to come today."

"Whoever it was may only have been trying to frighten me away, Mark. Once he got rid of his own thesis, along with the others, then he could assume that all connections to the murders were erased. He probably feels safe at this point. I believed Martin Harrison to be dead, and I certainly would not have guessed that he saved any papers after all these years, so that is what others must think, also."

Mark walked with Ellen along the corridor leading to the lower door of the Rotunda. It was a cold day, with tiny spars of sleet blowing in the wind. "Thank you for coming today." Mark took Ellen's hand into his own. "I don't know what I would do without your help—and Fannie's. It's just that I am worried about you. I'll be back in touch if I come up with anything new." For a moment, Mark put an arm around Ellen's shoulders protectively and held her close. Then, as if concerned by his action, he removed his arm hastily and hurried down the path.

Ellen watched as Mark walked away from her. She had become very fond of this young man and her feelings for him puzzled her. In one sense, she was attracted to him as a man. She could still feel his arm about her shoulders, and it gave her a warm sensation that she had not experienced in years. The feeling both surprised and pleased her. Imagine, at my age, she murmured to herself.

But, in another sense she felt about him as a mother, or perhaps even as the son-in-law she might have had if her daughter had lived. Ellen smiled ruefully to herself. If her daughter had lived and if her own life had not changed so dramatically, her beautiful, first-family-of-Virginia daughter would never have wed a man who grew up in Belmont, whose mother was a cook and whose father tended horses. The Ellen she once was would not have welcomed such a possibility. In fact, that Ellen would not have approved of the person she had become. She would not have a friend like Fannie, and she would not be involved in a murder case and, looking at her watch, she most certainly would not have been hurrying back to work so that she would have money to pay the rent.

CHAPTER THIRTY-ONE

I am now awaiting a person who, although perhaps not the perpetrator of these butcheries, must have been in some measure implicated in their perpetration.

—Poe's "Murders in the Rue Morgue"

It was a rainy morning, several weeks later. Fannie and Ellen were sitting in front of the fire, enjoying hot biscuits and butter.

"Fannie, we absolutely have to stop eating all of these rich pastries. I could hardly get my skirt buttoned this morning."

"You eat enough rabbit food and yogurt the rest of the week to cancel out the calories in this." Fannie laughed. "Besides, I just couldn't get biscuits off my mind this morning, and I had to get up early and make this batch."

"They are wonderful, Fannie. The best I have been able to do is mix up drop biscuits out of a quick mix."

"Well, anything that claims to make biscuits quick can't have much going for it. Biscuits have to be rolled and cut, or they just aren't really biscuits. But what these need is sausage gravy poured over the top. Now, that's something special."

Ellen grimaced at the very thought of the calories in sausage gravy, but she admitted to herself that the idea was appealing.

"Have you heard anything new from Mark?" Fannie asked, pouring herself and Ellen some more coffee.

Ellen had told her friend everything about Martin, after clearing it with Mark. After all, she had reminded him, Fannie had a great deal to do with the progress that had been made so far. She also assured Mark that Fannie could keep any secret entrusted to her.

"So far, Martin hasn't come up with anything, but he tells me that he feels the answer is in his files somewhere, if he can only locate it. Etta Mae has been helping him go through all his filing cabinets and boxes and rearranging everything."

"She sure is fond of that old man," Fannie said. "He has asked her to give up her other employers and work for him every day, and I think she's going to do it. She is also making arrangements with our cousin, Tom, to come in two or three times a week and help him with his bath and a shave and whatever else he may need. Etta Mae says he's getting around better every day and just itchin' to start seeing some of his old friends."

"Mark still has him under tight cover, for his own safety. If the murderer knew that Professor Harrison was still alive and, in fact, assisting with the investigation, his life could be at risk. I have been stopping over every day or two and I must say it is wonderful to have him back." Ellen smiled.

"Now, don't you go getting any romantic notions about that old fellow. He is just not up to the likes of you."

Ellen laughed. "I don't think that I could keep up with the likes of him. It has made me realize how cut off from people I have become. My work and the students have been my whole life—and my friendship with you, Fannie."

"Haven't I been trying to tell you that you need to get out more and see people? You're still young enough to have some men friends. Get dressed up, and go out on the town once in awhile. You're a good-looking woman and you should have you some fun. I know I still do." Fannie smiled wickedly.

"Let's get off of this subject before you start telling me about your love life," Ellen laughed. "We need to get this case out of the way so that Martin can come out of hiding."

"You know, if there was some way to get all of the suspects together in a group and then confront the murderer with the information you have, he might break. Sort of the way they always do in 'Murder She Wrote'," Fannie said. "All Jessica has to do is just present the facts and, the next thing you know, the cops are hauling the murderer off to jail, with the guilty party blabbing everything about the crime and beggin' forgiveness."

"Well, Fannie, real life is seldom as simple as just getting everybody together in a room and then having the murderer confess, as the cops step out from behind the curtains with the handcuffs," Ellen said. But Mark *has* mentioned the possibility of getting everyone together to see if he can solve the mystery of the vanished masters' theses. I'm going to offer the use of my house for a meeting place. Just maybe the killer will jump up and confess and then we can all go on with our lives."

CHAPTER THIRTY-TWO

The skies they were ashen and sober;
The leaves they were crisped and sere—
The leaves they were withering and sere . . .
—Poe's "Ulalume"

It was one of those Virginia winter nights that stunned those who had come to live in Charlottesville expecting to escape bitter weather. The temperature was about fifteen degrees, and there was a cold icy wind blowing that made the wind chill near zero. Ellen had built a fire in the fireplace and prepared mulled wine and hot cider. Mark was the first to arrive, planning to be there before the others, and he had arranged the chairs in the living room so that he could sit where he could see everyone.

"I hope something productive comes from this, Ellen. I still feel uncertain about possibly exposing you to this person again."

"Mark, I know all of these people. I am exposed to them already. Maybe something useful will come out of getting them together in the same room. Besides, you still have the police watching the house, in case you need a back-up."

Frank and Anne Gruver were the first to arrive. Ellen hung up their coats, and they sat down in the living room. There was an awkward silence. No one was sure how to handle themselves in this situation. Ellen saw that Anne was nervous and uncertain, and Frank reached over and touched her gently on the hand. Ellen wondered just how far this quiet man would be willing to go to protect this woman, with whom he was still so obviously in love. Ellen was offering them a warm drink when the doorbell sounded, and Mark went to let in Ted, who made a great to-do about removing his icy coat and rubbing his hands together over the fire.

"What a charming place you have, Ellen," Ted enthused. Ellen smiled and thanked him, thinking to herself that her small living room could not compare to the elegant houses on the Lawn but, then, the ever gallant Ted would probably have said the same thing if she were living in a homeless shelter. His was the trained reaction of those who usually find themselves in lovely rooms and hardly notice their surroundings. Ellen knew that Ted had gone to great lengths to preserve the illusion of a happy marriage. She wondered to what lengths he might go to protect his reputation and preserve the illusion of a gentleman scholar.

Ellen busied herself in the kitchen, preparing more drinks and feeling grateful not to be in the living room, when the doorbell rang again. She heard the voice of John Grieco and, even without seeing his face, she knew he was wearing his best political smile. He came to the kitchen to greet her, and Ellen was taken again with his charm and assured presence. He had learned the role of a confident leader very well. Ellen remembered him as a very reserved and painfully shy young man when he was a student of her husband. Tom had been concerned that he was not a particularly able scholar, but his dogged determination had kept him in the graduate program. Ellen also noted the impeccable tailoring of John's suit and the expensive silk tie. This man had done very well for himself—and he knew it. There were obviously benefits from being both a far-right Christian and a politician.

Ellen returned to the living room with a tray of steaming drinks, just as Sarah and her husband, Bennett Collins, arrived. It had been some time since Ellen had seen Sarah's husband, and she was reminded again of the sharp contrast between the two. Sarah was a vivacious and beautiful young woman, with the type of looks that could have led to a modeling career. Her husband was very quiet, and Ellen was ashamed to say that when she first met him she had stereotyped him as a withdrawn science nerd. It was only when he smiled that his eyes lit up behind the thick glasses, and he spoke with such genuine warmth and concern that Ellen had come to think of him as a most attractive person. Sarah hugged her mother and father and sat near them on the sofa. Even though Sarah and her husband could have had nothing to do with the original murder, they had both requested to be present, and Mark had agreed.

"It seems that we are all here, with the exception of Reverend Evans," Mark said, and at that moment the doorbell rang again, with two sharp bursts of sound that seemed to announce trouble ahead. Reverend Evans entered the room, with an angry expression on his face, tossing his coat on the stool. As he sat down, he began lashing out at Mark.

"I see no possible reason why we should be dragged into this unseemly mess. This should be police business, and you should take care of it. I am only here because my daughter and granddaughter are here. I really can't understand why you allowed this to happen," he glowered at Frank and Anne. "I forbade my wife to be a part of this because, as you know, she has not been well."

Ellen thought of Lydia Evans, the mousey little woman to whom he was referring, and wondered when she had last had an opinion of her own. She was what some would consider to be the perfect minister's wife—dedicated to her family and to the church. But Ellen had always felt that there was a sadness about her. Perhaps she had known, or at least suspected, the truth about her husband's secret gay life.

"I'm sorry you feel that way, Reverend Evans," Mark said, with great restraint. "This is not an interrogation. I asked you here because this investigation involves all of you, and we need your help if we are going to find some needed answers."

Anne spoke quietly to her father before he could protest. "I think that we should all be here, Father. This is not just police business. It is our business, too."

"Well, it certainly isn't any business of Sarah and Bennett. They weren't even born . . . ." He interrupted his own words, as though suddenly realizing what he had said.

"We asked to be here, Grandad. We know that this does involve me in a very significant way." Sarah spoke to her grandfather as though she had practice in standing up to him.

Reverend Evans sat back in his chair with resignation, and

Ellen recalled that he was in the same chair he had sat in the night he came to see her and tried to warn her not to pursue any inquiry. Ellen knew a great deal more now than she did on that day. She knew that this man was hiding a secret about himself that, in this conservative state and church, could ruin his life. She wondered how far he would go to protect not only his daughter, but himself and his lover, as well.

"I don't want to keep you here any longer than necessary," Mark began. We need your help with a problem in this investigation, and I believe that only you can give us the information we need. Let me put it directly to you. A major part of this investigation depends on our locating your masters' theses, or in Frank's case, the research he completed as a graduate student. We have reason to believe there is important information in one of those documents. All of them seem to have disappeared, including those of the two gentlemen who live, or in the case of Mr. Antonetti, 'lived' away from the area. Mark looked expectantly around the room.

"Well, surely you aren't suggesting that anyone deliberately did away with these documents," Reverend Evans interjected, less belligerently than before.

"Professor Mitchell," Mark said to Ted, who was noticeably uncomfortable, "Ellen tells me that she saw your thesis on the shelf some weeks after the murder of Charles Allan, but when she asked to borrow it later, you told her that it had been missing for years."

Ted Mitchell looked up in surprise and then, somewhat red-faced, he looked at Ellen. "I did tell you that, Ellen, and I am sorry. It just seemed better not to have my thesis under scrutiny."

"Well, *my* thesis really is missing," John Grieco spoke firmly. "When my life was changed by the Lord, I literally packed up many of the symbols of my old life, including copies of my master's thesis. However, when Reverend Evans spoke to me regarding the risks of having one's thesis scrutinized thirty years after it had been written, I could not have agreed with him more. Few pieces of research conducted when one is young and inexperienced can survive intensive scrutiny years later without some questions being raised, as he so accurately pointed out."

All eyes turned towards Reverend Evans, as John Grieco finished speaking. "Reverend Evans, did you tell people that they should hide their masters' theses from us?" Mark asked.

"I merely mentioned to people the risks of having research material picked apart so many years after the work had been completed. There are many examples of people's professional lives being ruined by having material written for a degree, when they were young, looked at with an adversarial eye many years later." He paused, defensively. "Anyway, I thought that if you didn't locate any of them you might stop all of this and let us alone."

"We are not adversaries in this, Reverend." Mark was obviously attempting to keep things calm. "We are trying to find out who murdered two young men. How did you find out that we were interested in the masters' theses?"

"Sarah mentioned to me that you were looking for Frank's notes, and I surmised that you must be interested in something that was written by these men when they were students. Then my friend, Mr. Perkins, mentioned that he had seen you in the library, Ellen, and that he was concerned because you seemed so upset. You asked him for the location of the masters' theses in English, I believe."

Mark looked at Ellen knowingly, and she knew that he was thinking of the many times he had warned her about speaking too freely to those in the library.

"This does not explain the disappearance of the material from our home," Frank Gruver spoke in bewilderment. "I certainly didn't have anything to lose by having that material studied. I never even completed the work for a degree."

Reverend Evans was looking at the floor, all signs of belligerence now faded. All eyes in the room turned to him as he cleared his throat. "I suppose that I must admit to having removed the material from Frank and Anne's home . . . ," he began, but he was interrupted by Anne, who moved across the room to stand behind her father.

"I know why Father removed those papers," Anne said. "He was trying to protect me from knowing the whole truth."

Her father looked up at her in some surprise and, Ellen thought, a certain dismay, as she continued.

"He thinks that I do not know about Henry Dodson and his blackmail attempt, but Frank told me years ago that Henry had threatened to deny he was the parent of my child and was trying to blackmail my father."

Ellen looked around the room and noted the expressions on the faces of the others after Anne had spoken. Ted had a shocked look of surprise on his face, since he had no idea that Sarah was the child of the murdered Henry Dodson. John Grieco had that look that politicians glue on their faces when they wish to remain sympathetically noncommital. Anne, Bennett, Sarah, and Frank had various expressions of sorrow and pain on their faces, for an old wound that had been reopened. The most interesting expression of all, however, was on the face of Reverend Evans, because it was one of barely concealed relief.

Ellen wondered if that relief was due to the fact that at least a part of his reason for having removed the papers was to hide a far more personal secret. Without the theses the inquiry would cease, and he would no longer be in danger of having his own "other" life investigated. It seemed very probable that Henry Dodson also had been blackmailing the good Reverend, and probably the vice chancellor, as well. For a moment, Ellen was tempted to confront Reverend Evans with the truth, but then something kept her from speaking. This man was weak and pompous and selfish, but she still did not want to be responsible for ruining his life.

Ted assured Mark that he would turn over to him the thesis on the following day and apologized again for having been so obstructive. Reverend Evans agreed to return the materials to his son-in-law to do with them as he pleased. In addition, Ted offered to call and speak to the others involved, requesting that they also send the theses, if they still existed. John Grieco reluctantly agreed to look again for his copy, but was still certain that he would not be able to locate it.

After they had left, Ellen and Mark sat before the fire discussing what they had experienced.

"Well, we now have the answer to the missing theses, but we are still a long way from having the answer to the murders."

Ellen wanted to tell Mark everything she knew about Reverend Evans and the vice chancellor, but, once again, something caused her to remain silent. What if she were protecting a murderer and not just a frightened, aging man? What if Bowman Ward was involved? Mark had no idea that he might have any connection with the murders.

Mark misread the concern on her face. "This has really been tough on you, Ellen. I think that perhaps I have asked too much of you."

"It's not that, Mark. I'm just concerned about these people whom I have known for years and the possibility that one of them is a cold-blooded murderer. I hope that I can help you get this over with. Let's hope that Martin will come up with something. One good thing that has come from this is that Martin has come back to Charlottesville."

* * *

The next evening, as Mark was working late in the office, the phone rang. "Don't touch anything. I will be right there." His hand trembling, he placed a call to Jake.

"What's the matter, Mark, has something happened?"

"It's Martin Harrison, Jake. Someone just tried to murder him."

CHAPTER THIRTY-THREE

But he grew old
This night so bold.

—Poe's "Eldorado"

"If I hadn't decided to come in and make sure the Professor was OK, I don't know what would have happened."

Tom hovered over the bed where Martin Harrison was propped up on pillows drinking a cup of warm milk.

"Tell me what happened, sir. Were you hurt in any way?"

Mark sat gingerly on the side of the bed and took out his note pad.

"I am quite recovered, thank you, Mark. There was no injury to my person. However, I must admit to being most upset by the incident. That individual certainly intended me most egregious harm. Had it not been for Tom's timely intervention, I am certain the individual would have succeeded."

Martin Harrison patted the warm dark hand that was smoothing the coverlet on his bed.

"Would you mind adding just a touch of brandy to this, Tom?"

"I want you to tell me exactly what happened, sir," Mark said. "When you have added that brandy, Tom, please go into the living room and give your statement to Sergeant Williams. It's a good idea to get the events from each of you separately."

Tom seemed reluctant to leave, but Martin Harrison assured him that he would be fine.

"I arrived home about 10:30 p.m. Tom had invited me to his cousin's home for dinner because he thought I should get out a bit. I have been sequestered here for quite some time. We did not wish to go to some establishment where I might be recognized, so he invited me to a family fish fry. His cousin makes the most remarkable fried catfish I have ever tasted. But I disgress. Tom walked me to the door, saw me inside and then left—or so I thought. The first thing I noticed was that someone had been going through my belongings. The desk drawers were open and papers were scattered on the floor."

"Was there anything missing, Professor?"

"I can't be sure, but I did not notice anything in particular having been removed. Just as I was about to call the police, a person emerged from the kitchen brandishing one of my carving knives."

"What did the person look like?"

"The individual was wearing women's clothes, a long dark coat, and low-heeled shoes with a hat pulled down low on the forehead. Oh yes, and wearing dark glasses. The glasses and the hat came together."

"Why do you say that she was "wearing" women's clothes? Do you doubt that the person *was* a woman?"

"I think the hair was really a dark wig. It was slightly askew. And the hands were those of a man. The person was wearing gloves, but the hands were large and so were the wrists. Of course, I can't be certain. It might have been a large woman, but my intuition tells me otherwise. I really could not see the face. The glasses were large, and the collar of the coat was turned up around the chin."

"What happened then?"

"I managed to interject a chair between me and my assailant. Of course, that would not have deterred him for very long. I fear that my ability to stave off attack is very limited. Fortunately, Tom had decided to return to make certain I was settled for the night. The sound of his key in the door caused the attacker to turn and make an escape through the rear service door, dropping the weapon in the process. We found where a pane of glass had been broken in the rear door where the intruder must have entered.

"The fact that the individual was using one of your knives makes me think that he or she did not bring a weapon in here intending to kill you. You probably surprised the person going through your things. He or she ducked into the kitchen and must have decided at that moment to take the knife."

"I have considered that point also, Mark. I don't think murder was the intention when he came—I shall refer to him in the masculine gender for the time being. I have the strong feeling that it became his intention just before he came through that door with the knife. He could have left when I arrived, but he must have decided that I needed to be eliminated."

"Tom said he found you on the floor. What happened?"

"Well, I am not a young man and I fear that my knees simply gave way. Tom has decided to move into the spare bedroom for the time being so that I will not be alone. I must affirm that such a plan gives me a great deal of comfort."

"We have been so careful not to alert anyone of your presence here. How can this individual have found out about you?"

Martin Harrison took a sip of the warm beverage and settled himself into the pillows.

"I am certain that it was not anyone who has been helping me. Every person that I know here has been most circumspect and I trust them with my life. There is some person we do not suspect who is giving information regarding my presence and my activities."

"We can't let this go on much longer. Now that more of my officers know of your whereabouts, it will be difficult to maintain any secrecy. I think that we had better end this and make it clear that you have no new information."

"Just allow me one more day. I feel that I am very close to determining the secret hidden in that text. If I do not succeed in twenty-four hours, then we will terminate the process and do as you say. In the meantime, I believe that Tom will remain by my side. He is a most comforting companion."

Tom came into the room with the officer, who had completed taking his statement.

"I have made arrangements for my youngest son, Clarence, to stay with us," Tom said.

Martin Harrison chuckled, "Clarence was a heavyweight boxer in the army. We should be well protected."

Mark smiled, in spite of his anxiety.

"You have certainly covered all the bases. OK—one more day and then we call it quits."

Mark shook the professor's frail hand and already regretted the agreement.

* * *

Ellen hung up the phone and turned to Fannie with a sigh of relief.

"Thank goodness, Martin is feeling just fine this morning, and he has both Tom and Clarence there with him."

"That attacker better think twice before he tangles with Clarence. He really is a sweet person, but I wouldn't want to take him on in a fight. Now, tell me more about what went on at the meeting the other night. With all this excitement about Martin, we haven't had a chance to talk more about it."

"I wish you could have been there, Fannie. It would have satisfied your enthusiasm for a 'Jessica' type of confrontation. The only difference was that the murderer did not confess."

Fannie poured some more hot chocolate in her cup and buttered a piece of homemade bread, topping it off with a large spoonful of homemade damson plum preserves—one of her specialties.

"At least you found out about the missing masters' theses. I hope that you're doing the right thing not telling Mark what you know about Reverend Evans and Bowman Ward. He's going to be very angry with you if this comes out and he finds out you didn't tell him."

"If I do tell him, Fannie, and he has to question these two individuals, it will not only ruin their careers, but it will be hard on Mark, also. I just don't think that these two men really are murderers, and I don't want to ruin their lives and, perhaps, Mark's career, as well."

"By the way, Etta Mae and Tom have been helping Professor Harrison go through his boxes. They say that he keeps finding all kinds of treasures in there."

"I know. He mentioned finding a note from William Faulkner, written when he was a writer in residence at the University, and also a paper that Katie Couric wrote when she was a student in his class." Ellen smiled, as she remembered the past.

"He has had a remarkable career. I think he is very happy to be back near the University and surrounded by the students he loves. People don't get over this place very easily. I don't think I would be happy living somewhere else, even though there are times when I would like to just walk away from all the turmoil."

"You're going to be walking away from the Rotunda pretty soon. Have you thought any more about what you're going to do?" Fannie helped herself to another slice of bread and a generous helping of cream cheese. "I know that I'm hanging up the mops and brooms very shortly, but I'm not ready to stay home all day and watch the soaps."

"I've been thinking more and more about that little tea room, and there just might be a way." Ellen hid her face behind the cup of chocolate, so as not to betray her excitement.

Fannie's face lit up with enthusiasm. "Honey, if you have found the money, I sure enough have the skillet and sauce pan. Are you serious, or is this just more day dreaming?"

"I told you that I have a little money saved, and I mentioned my idea to Martin. Well, he's very interested in becoming a partner, if we can work out the arrangements. Of course, this is still just an idea, but he was really very excited. He even came up with a name—Lenore's—after the lost love in 'The Raven.' He suggested we decorate the inside with enlarged illustrations from collections of Poe's work—particularly the illustrations in the old books."

"Praise be! I can feel my creative cooking juices flowing. Let's drink another cup of cocoa to seal the bargain. And then, let's get down to some serious planning."

CHAPTER THIRTY-FOUR

Each student is charged with the responsibility to refrain from dishonorable conduct. Accompanying this individual commitment to abide by the Honor System is an even more demanding commitment—a responsibility to ask those who violate our standard of honor to leave the University . . .

Explanation of the University of Virginia Honor System

Ellen was working at her desk late one afternoon the following week. A winter storm was blowing icy rain against the ancient glass of the rotunda windows and rattling the panes. Several times the lights flickered, as though a loss of power was imminent. Ellen was just about to turn off the lamp on her desk when the phone rang.

"I'll answer it, Marie," she called to the young woman who was sitting at the reception desk.

"Ellen?" It was Mark's voice and his excitement was evident.

"Yes, Mark, what is it?"

"Professor Harrison just called. He thinks he has found something that will be of interest. Do you want to go over there with me?"

"How about fifteen minutes? I'll be standing across from the library."

Ellen hurriedly put on her coat and galoshes and pulled a woolen cap over her hair.

"Bundle up warm," Marie called. "It is freezing outside. And be careful about the ice on the bricks. You can't see it, but it's there. I almost broke my neck coming back from lunch."

"I'll be careful, Marie. You had better close up shop and get home before the power fails. This is no time to be caught in the dark. Good night."

Ellen walked carefully down the brick path towards the library. The freezing rain was stinging her face, and she pulled the woolen scarf from her pocket and wrapped it around her throat. Students passed her, with their heads pulled inside their jackets like terrapins, bracing themselves against the storm. It had been a long winter, and spring seemed to have no intention of arriving early.

When they arrived at Martin's, they found him surrounded by papers and boxes, his eyes bright with excitement. "Please put another log on that fire, Mark, and bring that box of papers over to me." Martin indicated a particularly battered container.

"When I was teaching the Poe seminar, I felt very uncertain about the entire procedure, Ellen. My field of study is Tennyson, as you know. It was only because we were short a faculty member that your dear husband persuaded me I could handle this seminar and supervise the graduate students for a semester. He could talk the flowers off the wall, that man. If it had been my own field of expertise, I am certain that I would have recognized the textual material, but I simply was not that familiar with the Poe scholarship."

"What in the preface to the library book has alerted you, Martin?" Ellen asked.

"You see here, this long section in which the editor of this collection expounds the theory that Poe was deeply influenced in his writing by his stay at the University of Virginia. We know, of course, that Poe speaks explicitly of his experiences as a student in Charlottesville in the poem 'Tamerlane' and in 'A Tale of the Ragged Mountains.' The author of the introduction to this collection also proposes that these lines from Poe's poem 'Helen' may be an allusion to the Greek and Roman architecture of the Lawn.

> On desperate seas long want to roam,
> Thy hyacinth hair, thy classic face,
> Thy Naiad airs have brought me home,
> To the glory that was Greece,
> And the grandeur that was Rome.

He goes on to connect this poem with Poe's deep affection for a woman named Helen who befriended him as a youth and then died. This entire section in the introduction was torn from the book you found in the library, Ellen."

Martin leaned forward eagerly. "Now, here, it gets even more interesting, my friends." He held out the book so that they could both see where he was pointing.

"There is a footnote in this introduction referring to a series of letters that are now in the Poe collection in the library, but were known only to a very few people thirty years ago. The page on which this footnote appears was also torn from the book you located in the library, Ellen. In this footnote, the editor quotes from sections of those letters that confirm what he was stating in this introduction."

"That's right," Ellen exclaimed. "Susan told me that the Ingram collection is now in the rare books room. These were letters written to the man who wrote this preface, so he would have had the only first-hand knowledge of this connection. But, I still don't see how this relates to the masters' theses, Martin." Ellen was looking closely at the section in the text that had been torn from the original copy. "How will this information lead us to the murderer?" Ellen asked, as Martin Harrison began to rummage through a pile of papers in the box beside his chair.

"Just this, my dear Ellen. I saved a thesis written during the year that I taught the Poe seminar because the student cited this allusion, taking full credit for having made the connections to the University and to Poe's friend, Helen. I doubted very seriously that this particular student had the imagination or the sensitivity to come up with such an interesting surmise on his own. The student who wrote this paper goes into great detail to expound this theory in his thesis without giving any citation or acknowledgment of this material." Martin sat back and studied the paper in his hand.

"Even with my limited knowledge of the Poe material, I thought that something was amiss, but I could not prove that the student had taken his ideas from another source. The other members of his committee deferred to me in this matter, as gentlemen should, and, of course, the student insisted that this was his own work. As I said, I suspected at the time that these were not his original ideas, but I was not able to find where he might have obtained this information. Well, now we know."

"But it is just material taken from an old book. How could that be reason for murder?" Mark asked.

"It was a very foolish deceit. Only a student with a massive ego would take credit for the ideas of scholars and use their words as his own. With the single sanction in the Honor System, Mark, this plagiarism would have been considered stealing. The author of this thesis would no doubt have been expelled in disgrace. Your Henry Dodson obviously knew about this because the reference number to the library book was hidden in his secret box. For some reason, he must have threatened to use this information.

My friends, I believe we may have found your guilty party."

CHAPTER THIRTY-FIVE

While from a proud tower in the town
Death looks gigantically down . . .
—*Poe's "The City in the Sea"*

The election campaign for the state senate was nearing the end. There was a concerted effort by more liberal factions to unseat the two incumbents who were running for re-election—particularly one who was an outspoken proponent of the conservative Christian coalition—John Grieco. Grieco had waged an intense campaign, emphasizing the dangers of the liberal humanists who threatened the schools, especially those from the University of Virginia. He pointed out his success in having "decadent" material removed from the libraries and his dedication to seeing that public funds would be made available to private religious schools. Even his harshest critics agreed that John Grieco was a hard worker and a persuasive campaigner.

On Tuesday evening, the auditorium in the county high school was filled with people who had come to hear the candidates debate. The stage contained a lectern for the speakers, with a microphone and chairs for the candidates.

People milled about the room, and no one seemed to notice the addition of a few extra police. At five minutes after eight, the main speakers and those participating in the program walked onto the stage and took their places. The lights in the auditorium were dimmed. A member of the League of Women Voters, the organization sponsoring the debate, called the meeting to order and explained the rules of procedure.

Standing in the wings behind the side curtain of the stage, out of sight of the speakers, stood Mark Pace, with a tape recorder, and along the side wall near the press, dressed in plain clothes, was a detective, and Jake, with a video recorder. On the third row of the auditorium, just in front of the lectern, was Martin Harrison, wearing a look of eager anticipation. On the back row, in a far corner, were Fannie and Ellen.

"Well, you certainly got a room full of people for this performance," Fannie whispered, as the lights were lowered for the speeches.

Ellen, who was so nervous she had to grip the seat armrests to keep her hands from trembling, looked around the room. "Mark and Jake decided that this was the only way to possibly force a confession. It is melodramatic, but perhaps it will work. I think Mark has seated Martin so that a person on the stage would not notice him in the audience. Besides, it is difficult to see any individual in the audience with the lights shining on the lectern."

Each of the candidates spoke for fifteen minutes, and then there was a period of comments and rebuttal, before the lights were raised and the moderator opened the meeting for questions from the floor. The moderator had been informed by Mark that she should expect some unusual questions, and also that she should be sure to recognize the elderly gentleman seated in the third row at the end of the question-and-answer period. Many of the questions coming from the audience were directed at John Grieco, and he handled himself with great assurance and confidence. He was dressed, as usual, in the most impeccable taste, wearing a quietly understated, but very expensive grey suit and dark red tie. Grieco acknowledged to the audience that his positions were controversial in some quarters, but proclaimed that he was following the dictates of his conscience and his faith. To the query regarding why he thought that his conscience and his faith should be imposed on everyone, he smiled benignly and replied that sincerely-held beliefs were better than no beliefs at all, and that he wanted only what was best for "our precious children," to which the coalition members cheered enthusiastically.

"I have tried to live my life so that I could be an example to others," he intoned. "Moral virtue has been my guide and a lamp unto my feet."

"He can certainly lay it on," Fannie whispered to Ellen.

When most of the questioners had been recognized, the moderator pointed to Martin Harrison, who had raised his hand on a signal from Mark, whom he could see behind the curtain. Martin rose with great dignity and carefully placed his cane beside him. He seemed to be confident and in control.

"Mr. Grieco, perhaps you do not remember me, but I was your professor long ago at the University of Virginia, when you were a graduate student. My name is Martin Harrison."

John Grieco stared down at the man before him in stunned silence, as though he were seeing an apparition from beyond the grave.

"I was your faculty advisor when you were writing your master's thesis, Mr. Grieco, a copy of which I am holding here in my hand." At this point, he raised the document so that it was clearly visible to all in the room. Still, there was no reply from the candidate.

"It has recently come to my attention that portions of this thesis were taken directly from the pages of a rare book which was vandalized in the library. This is a copy of that book." Martin raised the book so that all could see. "You gave no credit to the author of the preface to this book, but took credit yourself for his ideas, and used his words as though they were your own. It seems to me that this constitutes a violation of the Honor Code at the University of Virginia. Under the rules of the Honor Code you would have been expelled for this offense, your graduate studies would have been terminated, and you would have left in disgrace."

John Grieco's face had turned red and the veins in his neck were protruding above the immaculate white collar.

"I have no idea what you are talking about. How dare you make such accusations regarding my morality?"

Martin Harrison had not lived for over eighty years, and handled any number of defensive students and irate faculty members, without achieving considerable aplomb.

"Two people have lost their lives because they knew of this plagiarism, Mr. Grieco."

The audience was murmuring in amazement at this unexpected

confrontation. People were turning in their chairs to look around the room, noting, for apparently the first time, the policemen standing along the walls. John Grieco stared at his old professor, standing so defiantly in the audience, and then, unbelievably, he smiled and stretched out his hands.

"Well, my dear Mr. Harrison, it is indeed a pleasure to see you again, even under these unpleasant circumstances. I must admit, however, you have taken me by surprise."

Then, he looked out at the faces in the audience and extended his hands in supplication. "My friends," he said, "as we grow older, we sometimes lose our—ah—perspective. My old professor was noted for his fine mind and brilliant scholarship. However, as his nephew disclosed just recently, he has been under the care of a physician for possible senility."

There was a hum of conversation in the room, and Martin Harrison seemed to collapse against the chair in front of him. Suddenly, he looked very old and very fragile.

"Your nephew was afraid that something like this might occur, and he informed the authorities so that you could receive supervision. He was also concerned that some others might use your—er—condition to further their own nefarious interests. It is difficult to believe what some will do to cause mischief."

At this, the murmur in the room turned into a clamor of angry voices, which Grieco silenced by raising his hands. "No, my friends, we must not give in to our anger or frustration. Professor Harrison and those who would take advantage of his weakness are to be pitied. We must go forward and be sure that the values we stand for are upheld by the voters in the next election."

With those words, John Grieco exited to thunderous applause, and Martin Harrison slumped into his seat with his hands over his face.

Jake came from the side of the room, lifted the old man from his seat, and helped him from the room before the press could reach him. As John Grieco left the stage, he smiled knowingly at Mark. "Very clever, young man," he said. "You simply made the mistake of misjudging human nature."

Mark was still standing behind the curtain when Bowman Ward materialized from the side entrance, his face contorted in anger.

"Congratulations. You have managed to embarrass a retired professor and make yourself look foolish tonight. I want to see you in my office first thing in the morning."

Standing at the back of the auditorium, Mark caught a glimpse of Dexter Paine, with a sly and knowing smile on his face, as he talked with the reporters about the "unfortunate incident." Mark was certain that he knew at last how the information about Martin's presence in Charlottesville had become known.

* * *

"Jake says that Martin is feeling better and now he is getting angry—particularly at that creepy nephew of his," Ellen said to Fannie, as she hung up the phone and sat down on the sofa disconsolately. "Martin told Mark he was treated for a while by a psychologist for depression and that he, himself, was fearful that he might be getting senile. The counselor prescribed some medication, which worked wonders, and advised him to seriously reconsider his intention of moving permanently to New Mexico, if he was unhappy there. It was at that point that Martin began to think about coming back to Charlottesville."

Fannie put her feet on the ottoman and took a sip of the hot tea she had prepared for both of them. "Sometimes I think a lot of people need to be protected from their own families when they get old." She paused a moment and said, "You know, I think I *will* spend the night here. It's getting late and you've had a bad time of it this evening. How in the world did that smooth-talking rattlesnake find out what was going on?"

"My guess is that Dexter Paine had something to do with that. He has gotten where he is today by toadying up to politicians, and this would certainly be a golden opportunity for him." Ellen took off her shoes and rubbed her feet. "Like Mark kept telling me, it's very difficult to keep anything secret in this town. Plus, the vice chancellor and Reverend Evans were certainly anxious to keep all of this quiet, as well. There is no telling what John Grieco knows about the two of them."

"Is there any chance that just telling the press what is known about that plagiarism is enough to get Grieco?" Fannie asked.

"Probably not. In the first place, it was many years ago that the honor offense was committed. John Grieco can simply plead ignorance of any wrongdoing or, at the most, say that he was sorry if he inadvertently copied material, but that 'little mistake' had nothing to do with the murders. It was a long shot to try to surprise him into an admission of guilt—and it didn't work. The evidence they have is all circumstantial. They would need a witness who could directly connect John Grieco to the murdered men. Plus, with that slimy nephew stating that his uncle was being treated for senility, Mark has lost his most important witness."

"Shoot! It looks to me like that man is going to get away with murder and get elected state senator in the bargain. Whoever said that justice was blind was right—blind, deaf, and dumb."

CHAPTER THIRTY-SIX

"Prophet!" said I, "thing of evil!—Prophet still, if bird or devil!"...

—Poe's "The Raven"

Mark walked back to his office, as depressed as he had ever been. The interview with Bowman had been worse than he had expected. Bowman had let him know that his work on the case had been unsatisfactory, and he was going to the Board of Regents and request that Mark be removed from his position. He said Mark had embarrassed the University with the fiasco at the press conference, and that he had been waging a vendetta against an important member of the state legislature. "You have never understood the nature of politics and compromise, Mark, and I am very disappointed in you. I was mistaken in assuming you could rise above your upbringing."

Mark realized for the first time that Bowman Ward had placed him in the position of chief because he believed he could control him. Far from "rising above" himself, he was supposed to behave like the son of a cook and a horse trainer and do as he was told by his "betters."

Mark could taste the bitterness in his mouth, as he thought of how proud he had been when he was selected for the job—how convinced he had been that he was chosen because of his ability and integrity. In reality, he had been chosen because he was broken and trained, and because he was anxious for that little cube of sugar as a reward for running around in circles. He had been jumping through hoops and standing on his hind legs for applause and recognition.

If had not been for Ellen, he would have obeyed Bowman and dropped the investigation. If she had not suggested looking behind the wall, the body of Henry Dodson would never have been discovered. Everything would have gone on as it had always gone on, and he would still be doing what he was told to do by his "betters." He was ashamed and, even worse, he understood what it was that had probably driven his wife away from him. He didn't know who he was or what he wanted to do. He was a phony and a failure. Thank God, it was finally over.

A car pulled up beside him and a familiar voice said, "Hey chief, how about a ride?" It was Jake. At first, Mark was reluctant to get in. He was feeling ashamed and betrayed and he wanted to go off and be alone. "Come on, get in, Mark. We might as well be miserable together."

Mark slumped into the passenger seat and stared out the window, as Jake drove to a nearby drive-in and ordered coffee for both of them. He pulled into a place in the parking lot and turned to face Mark. "Listen, I'm no great thinker and sometimes I can't figure out the simplest things about people, but I do know you're a good policeman. I know you are thinking that Bowman Ward has used you, but that's not true, Mark. For some reason he's a very frightened man, and he wants to blame you for his fear. Forget it, Mark. You are not responsible for what is bugging the vice chancellor. Let's talk about this case and what we know."

Mark sat up a little straighter and took a sip of the coffee. "Well, we know that some person has been feeding John Grieco information. My money is on Dexter Paine, but I can't prove it. John Grieco is a powerful man, and Dexter is very attracted to power." Mark rubbed his eyes. "I just can't believe that Dexter would assist a murderer."

"Dexter probably doesn't believe that Grieco is a murderer, or, at least, he won't let himself believe that possibility. I found out he belongs to one of the churches who give Grieco so much support in his 'crusades.'" Jake finished his coffee and put the cup in a trash bag on the floor. "To give the devil his due, Dexter probably does think there is some kind of evil conspiracy to trap John Grieco and keep him from saving us all from ourselves. How do you like being a major player in a conspiracy theory?" Jake asked, as he punched Mark lightly on the shoulder.

"I wonder what Grieco intended to do to Ellen in the library, if that was who stalked her in the stacks. And how did he know she was there?" Mark's hand clenched into a fist, thinking of the danger people he cared for had been in.

"Susan Blake, who works in the library, told me that Dexter had been in her office the day you discovered the damaged book. Maybe Dexter has been feeding information to Grieco. I wouldn't put it past him. It may have been coincidental that he was in the library when Ellen came, or he may have been the one calling her office who was told by the staff that day she was going to the library."

"It is possible that he hadn't finished hiding or destroying the theses, and he hurried over when he knew where Ellen was going." Mark drank the remainder of his coffee, not noticing that it had become cold. "You know, Jake, he might have killed her that day in the library."

Jake grinned as he turned toward Mark. "Thank goodness he underestimated what a tough lady she really is. He probably thought she would swoon away with fright."

"And what about Martin Harrison? Was it Grieco in his house that night? Once again, we could have had a murder, except for the bravery of a fine old gentleman."

"A real lady and a fine gentleman. They make quite a pair."

CHAPTER THIRTY-SEVEN

And the fever called "Living"
Is conquered at last.

—Poe's "For Annie"

When they reached Mark's office, Jake decided to come in for a few minutes and go over their notes once again. The secretary looked up with sympathy and concern as they entered and motioned in sign language that someone was waiting in the office. Mark's first response was irritation. Didn't she know better than to let anyone in? It was probably the press, who had been hounding him since the meeting.

He opened the door, prepared to dismiss whoever might have invaded his privacy, when he was startled to see Lydia Evans, Reverend Evans' wife, seated by his desk.

She was drawn up in the chair, as though to protect herself from attack. Her face was the color of washed ashes, and she looked as though it was taking all of her effort to remain upright. Mark hurried to her side. "Is there anything I can get for you, Mrs. Evans? You don't look well."

"No, Mark, there is nothing you can get for me—well, perhaps a drink of water." Jake rushed out to the cooler and returned with a paper cup, which Mark held for her as she sipped.

"I am not well, Mark. Most of the time now I'm in bed, but I felt a little stronger today, so I got dressed and called a taxi." She was short of breath and Mark took her hand in concern.

"Should I call your husband or your daughter? Perhaps you would feel better if they were here."

"No, Mark." She shook her head. "I came alone because I want to talk with you. I'm glad that Jake will be here, also, when I tell you what I have come to tell you." She paused for a breath. "I think you should record this, Mark."

When they were seated at the table and Mark had turned on the tape recorder, Lydia Evans began to tell her story.

"I knew that Henry Dodson had been seeing my daughter and that she was pregnant by him. My husband told me that Dodson was threatening to blackmail him and claim that the child Anne was carrying was not his. I called Henry Dodson and asked him to meet me in one of the gardens. When I pleaded with him about the blackmail attempt, he told me that all of the blackmail which he had been involved in had been masterminded by another person." She paused for a sip of water. "Henry needed money for tuition and had gradually become involved in the blackmail. He told me that he had fallen in love with my daughter and that he wanted to get out of the whole business. He was going to tell the other person—his co-conspirator—that he was through with all the blackmailing and that he wanted my husband and my family to be left alone, since he intended to marry Anne. Henry also told me that he and the other person knew something about my husband, personally—something that my husband would want to keep secret."

Lydia paused for another sip of water. She signaled to Mark to turn off the recorder. "Mark, I think I know what the 'something' was, but I don't wish to have it an official part of this record."

"Why don't you finish the story, Mrs. Evans, and then we can decide if you should tell any more than is necessary." Mark turned off the tape recorder.

"I have heard my husband and Bowman talking, and I believe that years ago they had an affair. Perhaps it has ended—perhaps not. I simply haven't wanted to know about it."

Mark tried to keep the surprise from registering on his face, and he could see that Jake was having the same struggle.

"Henry Dodson saw them together at the country club and so did the other blackmailer. They were using that information against both men."

Mark placed his hand on Lydia's arm. "If we can, we will try to keep this from coming out. I can't promise anything—except that I will try." Mark turned the tape recorder back on and she continued.

"I asked Henry how, when he ended his part in the whole business, he could keep the other person from continuing to blackmail my husband and others. Henry told me that he had something on his partner that would prevent him from continuing the operation. Henry said he had proof that the other blackmailer had plagiarized material in his thesis and that he would expose him if he didn't stop."

Lydia Evans stopped speaking and tears began to streak her cheeks. "He told me that he was going to tell me the name of the other man, just in case something happened, but that I was not to tell anyone else this story, unless it was absolutely necessary. I'm afraid I convinced myself for many years that it was *not* absolutely necessary."

Jake muttered under his breath, "Well, I'll be damned."

"A few days later," Lydia continued, her voice becoming more faint, "Henry was exposed in the media by one of the students he had blackmailed, and then he disappeared. I didn't know what to think. At first, I was so worried for Anne, and I couldn't imagine what had happened to Henry. He appeared to be sincere when he professed his love for her. I was afraid that the other person involved in the blackmail schemes had silenced Henry because he had obviously been fearful for his life when he spoke to me." She paused and took a deep breath. "Henry wanted to change and stop the blackmailing and in doing so he became a threat to a very dangerous and ambitious man. When Henry was exposed, his partner must have been fearful that the entire story would come out, including the plagiarism. Then, Frank Gruver came forward with his proposal of marriage to Anne and everything seemed to be working out. My husband was less anxious, so I assumed the blackmail threats had ceased. I decided not to say anything."

"What changed your mind, Mrs. Evans?" Mark spoke softly, in order not to upset the fragile woman.

"I realize now that by remaining silent, I was partly responsible for that poor young man's death." A sob escaped from her, and Mark moved quickly to make her more comfortable. "Also, I realize that a very evil man is serving in public office and corrupting those around him. I heard what happened to Martin Harrison, a man I always admired. I just can't let it go on any longer. The name he gave me was John Grieco."

"This information confirms what we have suspected, Mrs. Evans. Do you know who has been giving information to John Grieco?" Mark asked.

"I can't be certain, but I believe Dexter Paine has been keeping everyone informed of your actions. I have heard my husband and Bowman talking downstairs, when I was supposed to be sleeping. I believe Dexter was giving information to Bowman and to John Grieco."

Mark was furious that Dexter would have acted against him and that Bowman Ward was aware of his behavior.

Lydia Evans put her hand over his. "Mark, I don't have very long to live. I don't want to leave my family with a legacy of disgrace. Whatever you can do to protect my loved ones, I ask that you do it. You are a good person, and you know what it means to have sorrow and loss."

Mark stood up and went to the window to hide his feelings.

"I will do whatever I can, Mrs. Evans. But John Grieco must be brought to justice. I will need your testimony."

"And you will have it, Mark. But, I ask that you let me sign whatever papers are needed today, because I don't know about tomorrow."

Lydia Evans died two weeks later.

CHAPTER THIRTY-EIGHT

O, human love! Thou spirit given,.
On Earth, of all we hope in Heaven.
—*Poe's "Tamerlane"*

Spring seemed on the way at last, and the daffodils were poking up little green shoots on the patio in front of Ellen's house. Fannie had been dozing in the warm sunlight pouring through the front window, when Ellen came in from the kitchen carrying a tray of thinly sliced toast spread with low-fat cream cheese.

"What is this?" Fannie roused herself and glared at the toast with suspicion. "Are you suggesting that this is our Saturday morning special? Charred cardboard smeared with face cream?"

"Don't criticize before you've tried it. We have to serve something low in calories in our tea room. I found this recipe in 'Eating Light and Loving It.'"

Fannie eyed the proffered treat suspiciously and, after one bite, put the remainder on the plate and stood up. "Get your coat on. We are going to walk down on the mall, sit in the sun, and have something lovely from the bakery."

Ellen looked at her creation with resignation. "I have to admit, it didn't taste too good to me, either." She got her coat and the two walked along the sidewalk toward the mall, already busy with Saturday morning strollers eager to enjoy the first warm weather.

"Don't worry about making low-fat treats. I can come up with some choices that are tasty and won't do too much damage. The main thing is portions. We can serve reduced portions for those who want to eat less, but we don't have to sacrifice good taste. People come out to eat to have a treat, not a treatment."

"I suppose you're right. That certainly smells good." Ellen

sniffed the scent of warm baked goods, as they found a seat at one of the tables in front of the bakery.

They ordered coffee and two muffins and then sat quietly, watching the parade of people walking on the downtown mall—teenagers with their hair in green spikes and multiple holes in their ears, and probably other places too painful to mention; youngsters on their way to the ice-skating rink, with their skates slung over their shoulders; young parents pushing strollers; and elderly couples, walking quietly in the warm sun.

"What a pleasant place this is. I wouldn't live out in one of those dreadful suburbs if they gave me a house rent free," Ellen said.

"Well, I prefer the country, myself, but those suburbs are moving closer to me all the time. Every month, they seem to bulldoze another stand of trees or tear down another farmhouse." Fannie moved her chair under the shade of the large trees that were planted along the center of the mall.

When they had finished with their muffins and wiped away the last crumb, Ellen leaned back with pleasure and a smile of relief.

"What do you think about looking for a small space here on the mall for our tea room? Somewhere up there around the fountain might be nice. We need to start on our planning soon. If I retire this year, then we could be open next summer. Martin has already told me that he's spoken to his financial advisor about investing in our business. I think he intends to come down and entertain the customers when we open. He told me that he plans to tell a lot of senility jokes."

"You know, Mark told me that his mother was interested in helping out sometimes," Fannie added. "She is one great cook and it wouldn't hurt to have somebody besides me in the kitchen." Fannie smiled at Ellen's discomfort. "Never mind, I don't expect you to cook. You just get out in the front with Martin and add class to the place—and total up the profits."

"At least, we don't have to worry about the murders anymore. Mark thinks they have enough to send John Grieco to a different government institution than the state senate. Life will soon be getting back to normal for the people in this case, but the pain has been terrible. Anne and Sarah lost Lydia Evans, and Anne told me that she realized she never really knew and appreciated her mother's courage until she told her story."

"Well, maybe it was courage," Fannie humphed, "but too many southern ladies looked the other way and pretended they didn't know what the men folk were about. They pretended they didn't notice those slaves looked just like daddy."

"Well, it may have been late in coming," Ellen sighed, "but her testimony finally led to justice. Lydia Evans' signed statement regarding Grieco's involvement in the blackmailing, together with Martin Harrison's description of the plagiarism, was enough for a conviction."

"Well, you and Tom and I know that it wasn't really the whole story," Fannie interjected. "It has not come out that the vice chancellor and the preacher were lovers. It was reported only that Grieco knew about some 'indiscretion' involving the two of them, but it was never stated publicly what that was. Anyway, the vice chancellor plans to retire and move to Florida." Fannie clapped her hands in amusement. "I understand that Jake, of all people, had a private chat with Bowman and helped him to see the wisdom of a quiet retreat. I would really like to have observed good old Jake when he hiked up his suspenders and sat down to have a heart-to-heart with Bowman Ward."

"Reverend Evans is back in the pulpit, as though nothing ever happened. He is something else." Ellen shook her head in disbelief. "He apologized to the congregation and made it sound like he had a momentary fling—a 'youthful indiscretion.' I wouldn't be surprised if he is soon back to gay-bashing and passing his moralistic judgements on the 'wicked of the world.'"

"The one good thing that came out of this for Anne was that she discovered that Henry Dodson really did love her and that he wanted to marry her," Fannie said. "I hear that Anne has started fixing herself up and just seems to have more of her old spunk back."

"That came as a great relief to both Anne and Sarah," said Ellen. "Isn't it strange how something that happened so long ago could have such an effect on a person's self-confidence?"

"That weasel, Dexter Paine, may finally get his comeuppance. Rumor has it that Mark may be the next chief of police in the city."

"There are a lot of police officers who would celebrate that occurrence. It would be a wonderful thing both for him and for the city." Ellen did not add that with Mark working downtown and his mother in the tea room, she might have an opportunity to see him more often.

"How did that poor boy, Charlie Allan, ever let himself be tricked into that room? I can't imagine crawling through the dirt in the dark and then being alone in that spooky place."

"John Grieco is a very persuasive person, as we know. He appealed to Charlie's enthusiasm for Poe's writing with the Amontillado wine and the reading from 'The Raven.' Charlie must have followed the initiation rites he had found in the box and climbed into that room from the crawl space, replaced the trunk over the opening, and underlined the verse from *The Raven*. At the signal from Grieco outside the plexiglass door, Charlie drank the poisoned wine Grieco had left there and called out, "Quoth the Raven, Nevermore!"—his last words. Ellen shivered at the cruelty of the murderer. If poor Charlie had only guessed what was hiding behind that bricked-up passageway, he might have gotten a different message from Poe's story. There was an indication that Grieco had poisoned Henry Dodson before placing his body behind the wall. Mark told me that Charlie's mother finally had the courage to look through his things. She found a diary in which Charlie mentioned that John Grieco was helping him to recreate the secret society and he was excited about his 'initiation.' His mother took some comfort in the fact that Charlie had not taken his own life."

"What did they find out about that cross-dressing?"

"Mark told me that John Grieco's secretary came forward with an outfit of women's clothing that matched those of the person seen outside the Poe room and in Martin's apartment, including a dark wig and hat. She had noticed them under a box in the supply cabinet some months ago and had become suspicious. When the news broke of Grieco's arrest, she brought them to Mark. Apparently, there were a number of things she had noticed about Mr. 'Holier-than-Thou' that were helpful in the case. For instance, she knew that Grieco had taken Charlie to dinner several times. Once, she picked up the phone and heard Grieco and Dexter Paine discussing "the matter in the library." He was probably dressed in some kind of disguise when he was stalking me in the library that day. That was the way he got in and out without being recognized."

"Do you think Grieco would have harmed you in the library, Ellen?"

"I honestly don't know. It's possible that he only intended to frighten me, but I had a terrible feeling in there. I'm fortunate that I never had a chance to find out. After all, he murdered twice in order to protect himself, and I'm sure that he would have been willing to do so again. Martin is certain that he was going to use that knife when he was in his apartment. Grieco must have come in searching for the book, but he seemed willing to kill when Martin surprised him. Oh dear, let's get off this subject. I'm just glad that everyone can get back to leading their normal lives."

"Well, I can think of one person that hasn't really gotten back to normal." Fannie leaned toward Ellen with a serious look on her face.

"Who are you talking about—not me—I'm fine." Ellen looked at her friend with astonishment. "What makes you think that anything is wrong?"

"Well, first you've stopped going to church, and I know that your church has always been important to you."

Ellen sighed with resignation. "I guess that's true, and I do miss the service, but there is no way that I can worship in a church with Reverend Evans in the pulpit. It's not because of his past, but because of his life of deception, and the harm he has done to those who love him."

"Well, don't go back there. Come with me to my church for a while, until you find the right place. We're a country church; mostly black and fundamental; but we are also a loving group with a kind minister and the best music in the county. Oh, I know." Fannie acknowledged Ellen's look of concern. "You are Episcopalian to the bone and you are going to find your way back to the incense and the kneeling benches. But, in the meantime, come with me."

"Thank you, Fannie. I may do that. I miss being part of a church community, but I'm just not sure yet where I need to be. So much is changing in my life. I'm not sure about myself these days."

Ellen thought, but did not say out loud, how much she missed seeing Mark. But he had other business and a life of his own. Working with him had been exciting and she enjoyed his company. In some ways, he made her think of the years she had missed without an interesting man in her life.

"I notice that you don't wear that locket anymore. Did you lose it?"

"No, it's in a box beside my bed and I look at it every day." Ellen smiled softly. "It just seemed the right time to put the past aside a bit. After this experience, I realize that fear and loss are a part of life, just as courage and love are, also. There is one thing I forgot to tell you, though. I signed up for driver training last week, and I have been looking at automobiles."

"Hallelujah! Some new doors are opening for us, my friend. The Lord is not finished with these two old girls yet."

Fannie and Ellen smiled together in the warm sunshine.

Quoth the Raven, Nevermore!